AXEL

SINGLE DADDY SHIFTERS #1

TASHA BLACK

13TH STORY PRESS

13th Story Press

PO Box 506

Swarthmore, PA 19081

13thStoryPress@gmail.com

TASHA BLACK STARTER LIBRARY

Packed with steamy shifters, mischievous magic, billionaire superheroes, and plenty of HEAT, the Tasha Black Starter Library is the perfect way to dive into Tasha's unique brand of Romance with Bite!

Get your FREE books now at tashablack.com!

AXEL

1

AXEL

Axel Swann took a deep breath, anticipation building in his chest as the change took hold. He let the air out with a whoosh, his whole body expanding as he dropped to all fours.

By the time his hands hit the lawn, they were no longer hands.

Tender blades of grass tickled the pads of his massive paws.

He shook his thick pelt and lifted his snout to the swollen moon, drinking in the delicious sounds and smells that rushed toward his enhanced senses.

Fall had begun working its magic on the landscape. The colorful leaves still held fast to the trees, but he could practically hear their stems loosening, and he could taste the edge of cold in the fresh night air.

He loped off towards the trees, yearning for the scent of pine that his paws would kick up. His muscles sang as he leapt.

He had so few chances to indulge the beast within, and it had been so long...

"Hal, is that *a bear* in the neighbors' yard?" a woman's voice called from the deck next door.

"It's not a bear," the husband yelled back in a bored way.

"I think it's a bear," she repeated.

"Edith, it's *not* a bear," he said. "We live in the suburbs. There's no bear."

Axel froze, holding his breath.

There was a loud crackle of static, followed by the faraway sound of wailing.

He sighed, and let his body shift back to its human form.

The scents and sounds faded.

And his sense of fear returned.

Shit.

He scuttled back to the house, grabbing his bathrobe from the back porch in one hand and the baby monitor in the other.

He managed to get inside and lock the door before Edith could come over to investigate. But he knew she'd be over in the morning to tell him all about the animal she'd spotted in the yard.

He ran a hand through his hair and shook his head.

Shifting at home was a risk. The backyard was so small - just a wooden fence, and an expanse of lawn with a stand of pines in the back.

But it wasn't like he could go anywhere else.

No matter how seductive the call of the moon, Axel would never leave the radius of that baby monitor.

He placed the monitor on the kitchen table and pulled on his robe, tying it firmly around his waist.

The baby had quieted, but Axel would check on him anyway. He liked any excuse to visit Noah in the night.

The doctor had told him not to hold and feed Noah so much if he wanted him to sleep through the night, but it was difficult to let the little fellow cry alone in his own room. Given their situation, Axel figured he'd rather err on the side of indulging him.

He moved through the dining room, still decorated with his ex-girlfriend's frilly tablecloth, through the living room with his big chair and small fireplace, and up the creaky stairs.

Noah's door was the first one at the top of the steps.

Axel stood in the hall for a moment, listening.

No sound came from inside, but he wrapped his big hand around the knob anyway, and closed his eyes before easing it open, as if not watching the door might make it quieter.

The room was filled with Noah's sweet scent. Technically, Axel knew it was mostly the scent of baby powder and the delicate detergent he used to wash the baby's sheets and clothing. But there was an undertone of pine and cinnamon he swore was the woodsy scent of his little one.

Noah was asleep again, his little body splayed on the crib mattress, tiny hands open wide like stars, the moonlight from the window playing up the dimples of his chubby cheeks.

His tiny eyebrows were slightly furrowed, as if he disapproved of whatever he was dreaming about.

"It's okay, buddy," Axel half-whispered, half-sang, caressing his son's pillowy cheek with a calloused index finger. "Daddy's right here. Daddy will never leave you."

Noah smacked his lips in his sleep and his forehead smoothed.

Axel felt his heart melt, for the millionth time.

"My boy," he whispered.

Axel stayed just where he was for a long time before finally sneaking away for his own night of sleep.

The next morning, he woke up early and headed to the Tarker's Hollow Community Center, as planned.

The air was crisp and fragrant, and Noah was making happy growling noises.

"You're excited to see your friends, huh, buddy?" Axel murmured to him as he dug in his pocket for the keys to the building.

He and Noah enjoyed their mornings at the baby playgroup once a week.

Axel had volunteered to open up the place and clean up the toys at the end, hoping to get in good with the tight group of stay-at-home moms who seemed to run everything in town. After all, Noah would be going to school with their kids one day - Axel needed to prove he was a trustworthy presence for playdates.

But so far it hadn't seemed to win him much goodwill. No matter how friendly Axel was, the women hadn't taken a shine to him. The other single dads in the group had theories on that, but Axel didn't like to presume. He hoped that in time he would be accepted.

Balancing Noah on his left hip, he opened the door and jogged up the stairs to turn on the lights.

The huge arched windows that lined the north side of the room looked out over verdant views of the Tarker's Hollow College campus and soccer field.

The space used by the playgroup was as big as a ballroom. It had been used for the high school's required dance classes back in the fifties, as his great-aunt liked to remind him.

Now, it was mainly rented out for parties and used by the playgroup twice each week. Axel could only afford to close the shop one morning each week to attend with Noah, but his buddies Dax and Chase came Wednesdays and Fridays with their kids.

He opened the big closets on the near side of the room and pulled out a nice selection of toys for different age groups.

Noah was too little to do much more than lie on a play mat and kick his legs, but the toddlers at playgroup used the bikes and the toy kitchen and other items they cycled through week by week.

Satisfied with the offerings for the "big kids," Axel lowered his backpack to the floor, opened it with one hand and pulled out a fuzzy blanket. He spread the blanket on the floor and sat down with Noah just as heavy footsteps jogged up the stairs.

"There's Noah," a voice boomed.

"Hey, Chase," Axel said with a grin. "And hello, Jacob!"

Chase Bowman always brought his nephew to play-group. His sister worked a nine to five in the city and Chase's job fundraising for the college meant he sometimes worked late nights. He'd told Axel that when he'd asked for flex hours so he could spend mornings with his nephew, the dean had granted his request on the spot.

"How are you guys?" Chase asked, spreading out his own blanket and sitting down with little Jacob.

"We're great," Axel said.

"You look tired," Chase said sympathetically. "Were you out late last night?"

Axel knew they were alone, but he glanced around out of instinct before replying.

"I can't really run with the moon these days," he said. "I tried last night, but the neighbor yelled something about bears and then Noah woke up..."

"Wait—*what*?" Chase asked.

"Well, I try to be quiet, but the yard is so small..." Axel began.

"You tried to shift in your *yard*?" Chase asked, incredulous. "Dude, that's hilarious!"

"It's not hilarious," Axel said, though he was pretty sure Chase was right and he was just too grumpy to see it. "What am I supposed to do? I can't leave Noah."

"Why didn't you call Hannah Harkness?" Chase asked, as if it were the most obvious thing in the world. "She watches him all the time."

"Who watches him all the time?" Jenny Wilks-Andrews asked brightly from the stairwell.

Chase's eyebrows shot up.

Jenny was a shifter too, so her hearing was enhanced. She was also a stay-at-home mom and thick as thieves with the little clique of mostly human moms that ruled the roost at play group.

"Hannah Harkness," Axel said. "How's it going, Jenny?"

"Great," she said firmly. "Daniel is having a pleasant day, right, Daniel?"

"Horse," Daniel trumpeted and galloped over to the rocking horse Axel had set up by one of the windows.

"He's getting so big," Axel said, shaking his head in disbelief.

"He's only in the eighty-seventh percentile," Jenny barked out defensively.

Dear Lord. He had done it again.

Axel could never seem to say the right thing with these women.

"I only meant he's so active and so tall," he said quickly.

But the damage was done, Jenny brushed her hands together as if she were washing herself clean of him, then took off for the top of the stairwell where her best friend, Megan had appeared with her newborn.

Chase rolled his eyes and Axel smiled. At least Chase understood.

"Anyway," Axel said. "Hannah's only in high school. It's fine for her to watch Noah during the day when I'm at the shop. If anything goes wrong, I'm in shouting distance. But not at night. Besides, summer's over - she went back to school this week."

"What are you going to do?" Chase asked, his eyes full of sympathy.

The opening bars of *Hungry Like the Wolf* rang out suddenly.

"Oh, man, that's my phone," Chase said, slipping it out of his pocket and swiping with his thumb. "Dax is here, hang tight."

"You can stay with Uncle Axel," Axel told baby Jacob, who was sitting up in his boppy-pillow, wriggling his fingers and chuckling at a fascinated Noah.

Chase jogged down the stairs and returned a moment later carrying one twin, Dax right behind him with the other.

"Soon they'll be walking up the steps," Axel said.

"From your lips to God's ears," Dax said. But he was smiling.

As far as Axel could tell, Dax tried to be smiling all the time. He had lost his wife the night she gave birth to the twins, but Dax was determined to solider on and give Maddie and Mason the happiest childhood possible.

They were almost a year old now, and it looked like he was smashing his goal. The twins seemed to be made of blond curls and drooly smiles.

"Bane is coming later," Dax said as he sat down with Maddie.

Chase sat Mason down on Dax's other knee and seated himself again.

More women came up the stairwell, greeting each other and cooing over the babies.

None came over to the sunny spot the guys had set up.

"Bane's back, huh?" Axel asked. "How does he seem?"

Dax shrugged. "He just lost his sister, and he wasn't exactly planning on a life in the 'burbs with a baby. But he sounded pumped to see us."

None of the men had planned to be single dads - or part-time caregivers, in Chase's case. But together they were bringing up some pretty special children, and learning to appreciate the privilege more every day.

"Welcome to Playgroup," Jessica McAllister's bright soprano voice chimed crisply. "Your first visit is free. Here's a form to fill out if you want to come back."

That wasn't her usual effusive spiel.

"Thanks," said a familiar voice.

"Bane," Chase called, looking over Axel's shoulder at the top of the steps.

"Please be very careful with those beverages," Jessica said with a frown. "We rent this space from the College."

"I guess Jessica's worried this whole place will be taken over by single dads soon," Dax whispered to Axel, his eyes twinkling with humor.

Axel turned to see Bane approaching with his nephew Oliver. He had one hand wrapped around Oliver's, the other held a flat of paper coffee cups.

Bane was tall, dark-haired, and covered in tattoos, though you wouldn't know it with the long sleeve t-shirt and jeans he wore today. Axel figured Bane was trying to make a good impression on the moms of Tarker's Hollow too.

Good luck with that.

"Look at your handsome nephew," Axel said. "You're getting so tall, Ollie."

"My handsome son," Bane said quietly. "The adoption went through last week."

Axel felt a pang at the mixture of pain and pride evident in Bane's deep voice.

"That's awesome, man," Dax said appreciatively. "Congratulations."

They all watched quietly for a moment as Oliver immediately began putting together a wooden puzzle. Ollie was a super smart kid - he was only a toddler, but you could already tell.

"So, what's new with everyone?" Bane asked.

"Axel's babysitter went back to high school this week," Chase said immediately.

"Oh wow, what are you doing for childcare?" Bane asked.

"I found a nanny through one of those services," Axel said. "She's coming into town today."

He held his breath, hoping his friends wouldn't judge him. He loved his son, but he had to work, and he couldn't keep asking his apprentice to babysit.

"What, like Mrs. Doubtfire?" Chase asked.

"Well, hopefully not exactly like that, but yeah," Axel laughed.

"Aren't there a dozen women in Tarker's Hollow who would love to help you with Noah?" Chase said with a playful wink.

"Very funny," Axel said. "I'm not looking for any kind of entanglement. I just want a professional."

There was a moment of awkward silence in which Axel cursed himself.

His friends knew he had some trust issues especially when it came to Noah. After all, the child's own mother had abandoned them.

"I think it's fantastic," Dax said quickly. "You could definitely use some live-in help."

"Isn't that kind of expensive?" Bane asked.

"It's less than you might think," Axel said. "And it's an investment in Noah's future. The service tells me she has a degree in early childhood development, and her references were amazing. Noah will be in great hands."

"But don't you have to, like, feed her?" Dax asked with a furrowed brow.

It was no secret that Axel was a terrible, bordering on dangerous, cook.

"They said for an additional fee she'll prepare meals," Axel said, "and even teach me to cook."

"Good thing she has that degree," Dax quipped.

"What?" Axel asked with mock offense. "I'm not *that* bad in the kitchen."

"No comment," Chase said, his eyes twinkling. "But the fire department might have a thing or two to say."

"Okay, that was *one* time," Axel admitted.

"Yes, but we almost died," Chase reminded him. "So it's worth mentioning."

"Okay, mommies," Jessica yelled in her cheerful nasally voice, completely ignoring the fact that there were dads and other caregivers in the room. "Time for music!"

"Here we go," Dax said, leaning into Bane. "Just try to keep up."

2

DELILAH

D elilah bit her lip and signaled a left-hand turn.

The sign for Tarker's Hollow indicated a shaded, tree-lined street. Hopefully the town wasn't too sleepy.

As soon as she pulled in, branches met overhead, forming a green canopy. Beautiful old Victorians peeked out at her from behind the dappled shade of the enormous trees and hedges.

She felt as if she were driving into another world.

Two women approached each other on the narrow side-walk, one with a dog, the other with a stroller.

Delilah glanced back at them, expecting a showdown.

But the dog lady stepped onto the grassy shoulder and the two waved to each other in the soft morning light.

Wow.

She'd been in the city so long, with nothing but concrete, glass and unfriendly faces. This town looked like something out of a fairy tale.

A person like Delilah didn't belong in a place like this.

Even the misty air tasted too pure.

A few minutes later she passed the Tarker's Hollow College campus and a little village came into sight. It was just a train station and a block or two of small shops. The library seemed to be the largest building in the whole town.

Delilah glanced around, anxious to find a mechanic or service station.

She had hoped she'd be able to dump the car at a big franchise, but that wasn't going to happen, which was too bad. Small town people asked too many questions. And this was a pretty fancy car.

But the low fuel light had kicked on when she was still on I-95, so she'd had to take the Tarker's Hollow exit and hope for the best.

The village shops passed by quickly, and she found herself back in the residential section. The trip had been a bust after all.

Just as she was about to give up hope, she saw the sign.

Swann Automotive

IT WAS A TINY SHOP. Behind it, a gravel road seemed to lead into the woods.

She pulled in, hoping she could drop off the keys without much conversation. The last thing she wanted was to be remembered.

Her heart pounded as she approached the door and read the sign on the other side of the glass.

CLOSED - PLEASE USE KEY DROP!

. . .

SHE CHECKED HER PHONE.

It was after 9 am, surely this couldn't be right. She was under the impression that all auto shops opened up at dawn. Just how sleepy was this town?

But there were no lights on, and the door was firmly locked.

Counting her lucky stars, Delilah dropped the car keys in the wooden drop box next to the door and looked around.

She could probably make it back into the little town center in ten minutes on foot. Hopefully, the change in her pocket was enough to get her on a train to Philadelphia.

From there, she just needed to find a place to lay low for a few days and she'd be home free.

She had found her way out of a con that had gone wrong.

She'd thought she was done for, but it looked like she was going to make it after all.

Just then, she heard the crunch of gravel as a car pulled into the lot.

Delilah spun on her heel, intending to try and get as far away as possible before the person got a good look at her. Hopefully it was just another customer, not an employee.

"Hey there," a masculine voice shouted, stopping her in her tracks. "You're early."

I am?

She thought for an instant about just bolting, but the car door was already opening, and a man was climbing out.

He was more of a mountain than a man, really - tall and burly, his blue eyes twinkling at her.

She smiled back instinctively, her mind racing as she vacillated between flight and fight.

You can't fight him. He's freaking enormous, a little voice in the back of her head said appreciatively.

But there was no time to ogle and no time to run, because the man had already gotten something out of the car and was heading her way.

"The service said you'd be here this afternoon," he called to her from the other side of the car. "I hope we haven't kept you waiting too long."

We?

She blinked back her amazement at the tiny bundle he carried.

He was carrying a baby - a baby that looked absolutely tiny in his massive arms.

"I haven't been here long," she ventured. She had no idea what he was talking about, but the first rule of a good con was not to ruffle the mark.

"I'm Axel," he said. "And, as you already know, this is Noah."

The baby gazed at her with large, blue eyes, just like his father's. His tiny lower lip was pushed out slightly and the swirl of silky hair on his head gleamed in the muted sunshine.

"Hi, Noah," she heard herself murmur. "I'm Delilah."

"Oh, shoot, here you go," the man said. "I should have introduced you properly."

He held out the baby, enormous hands wrapped around the tiny ribcage.

Delilah had never held a baby before, but she couldn't think of a way to decline. There was something decidedly alarming about seeing the tiny baby dangling in the air even in those big hands.

She took him in her own arms, where he still looked pretty small, and cradled him to her chest, wondering at the incredible scent of him.

He laid his head against her shoulder and she didn't

want to breathe for fear that she might startle him like a deer.

"He likes me," she whispered.

"Yeah, he's a good boy," Axel said tenderly. His voice was so deep it was almost a growl. "Let me show you the house."

She followed the big man down the gravel path that led behind the shop.

His impossibly wide shoulders narrowed at his waist and hips. He reminded her of the cartoon version of Tarzan she'd crushed on as a tween.

The path led not into the forest as she'd suspected, but to a little cottage with a covered front porch. It was the first in a line of three small homes that bordered the trees.

"I never had a nanny before," Axel said. "A high school girl was watching Noah for me this summer. I did my best with your room. You'll let me know if you need anything else in there?"

"I'm sure it's fine," she replied.

A nanny. He thought she was a nanny. It was starting to come together.

They walked through a charming living room with a fireplace and headed upstairs.

"This is Noah's room," Axel said, indicating the room at the top of the steps with handprinted wooden letters that spelled out the little guy's name."

Little as he was, Noah was feeling decidedly heavier in her arms after the trip up the steps. He had definitely seemed smaller when his enormous father had been the one holding him.

"My room is here," Axel said, pointing to the door next to Noah's. "And yours will be at the end of the hall."

He opened the door to her room and stepped aside for her to enter.

Bright sunlight greeted her from a bank of windows that extended on both side walls and across the front of the house into the branches of a huge maple. She felt as if she were in some kind of tree house.

A full-size bed in a simple white frame with a matching dresser next to it took up most of the room, though a cozy rocking chair fit perfectly in the far corner.

It was beautiful, maybe the most beautiful room she had ever seen.

"I know it's really small," he said. "It used to be a sleeping porch, but the former owner converted it. The house just isn't that big. It's only me and him, and now you..."

"It's perfect," she told him. "I love it." She looked around for a moment, pretending that she was really going to live here and sleep in this magical room.

But that wasn't the case. The real nanny would probably be along any minute. She had to figure out a way out of here before that happened.

"He's sleeping, isn't he?" Axel asked, looking down at the baby. "Here, I'll put him down this time."

He took the baby carefully from her arms, which suddenly felt empty and cool without Noah's sweet weight.

"I'm, um, gonna check out the living room again," she lied as she catapulted herself down the steps.

She was almost at the front door when the phone rang.

It wasn't a cell phone. This was a true, jangling ring, like the landline at her grandma's house.

"*Cozy Cradles Nanny Service*," the machine announced in a robot voice.

On pure instinct she grabbed the receiver.

"Hello," she said softly into it.

"Hi there, ma'am, this is Elaine from Cozy Cradles," said

a polite voice on the other end. "I'm very sorry to tell you this, but your nanny has the stomach flu that's been going around. We're working hard to find a substitute but with the fall weather there's a lot of illness, and we're stretched pretty thin."

"Oh, that's fine," Delilah said smoothly. "Don't bother with a sub for us, we'll be okay. What does she need? Just a few days before she can start?"

"Oh thank God," Elaine said in a relieved way. "Yes, just a couple of days and I'm sure she'll be ready to report for duty."

"That's just fine," Delilah said. "You have a nice day now, Elaine."

"You too," Elaine said happily.

Delilah hung up just in time to see Axel heading down the stairs.

"Was that the phone?" he asked.

"Yes," she said. "I saw it was my agency and I thought I'd better pick up, so the phone didn't wake the baby. They just wanted to make sure I made it here okay."

"That's very nice of them," Axel said.

"You picked a great agency, Mr..." she thought of the sign over the shop. He must be the owner. "Mr. Swann."

"I hope so," he said. "But please, just call me Axel."

"Axel," she echoed with a smile, remembering her mom's old obsession with '80s hair bands. "So the shop out front is yours?"

"Guilty as charged," he said with a smile. "I've always liked working with my hands.

It was hard not to think of what else he might like to do with those hands.

The living room suddenly felt very tiny and the space between them charged with electricity.

"So where are your bags?" he asked, clearing his throat.

"It's um, just this," she said, holding up her backpack.

"You don't have a suitcase?" he asked uncertainly.

"Oh, well I *did* have one," she lied. "But I left it on the train. I'm such an idiot. I'm sure I'll get it back."

"Was your cell number on your luggage tag?" he asked.

"Oh, I don't have a cell phone," she lied. All she needed was him asking for her number. She only had the burner phone from the con.

And no way was she giving him anything that could get him entangled in that mess.

It was bad enough that she had left the car at his shop.

"Want me to call Septa's lost and found?" he asked.

"Oh gosh, no, I'm sure you have work to do," she said. "Is it okay for me to use your land line to do that while Noah naps?"

"Sure," he said. "I guess it worked out that I had the landline for Hannah."

"Who's Hannah?" she asked, looking around for signs of a woman. If the baby had a mother, she might be more perceptive than Axel was. It could make it much harder to hide out here even for a day or two.

"She's the high school student who helped with Noah for the last month or two," he said. "She doesn't have a cell phone either."

"Okay," Delilah nodded, feeling better. He had told her it was only himself and Noah in the house. And now Delilah.

"Well, I'll be at the shop if you need me for any reason," Axel said. "Please make yourself at home."

"Thank you," Delilah said. "I will."

He had no idea.

Axel headed to the shop with a spring in his step.

She's just a nanny, she's here for Noah, not for you.

But it was impossible not to enjoy the afterglow of the simple conversation with Delilah.

It wasn't that she'd said anything particularly deep. He had hardly learned a thing about her. Frankly, she seemed a little nervous.

But he was moved by the careful way she held Noah, and the look of wonder in her eyes when she'd seen the tiny room he'd set up for her.

And Noah himself, who was in a phase where he was wary of strangers, had gone right into her arms. And apparently felt so secure in his decision that he'd gone promptly to sleep on her narrow shoulder.

These things made him feel like he already knew Delilah in the most important ways. She made his son feel safe. She appreciated the view of the treetops from her small room.

"What's got you smiling this morning?" his apprentice, Bill, said in an almost accusatory tone.

"The nanny's here," Axel said. "And Noah likes her."

"How do you even know she's qualified?" Bill demanded. "I can't believe you just left him with her."

Sometimes he thought Bill was more protective of Noah than he was himself.

"She's experienced," Axel said. "She has a degree in early childhood development, too. The agency found her for me."

Bill snorted, but kept his mouth shut.

"I think she's amazing," Axel heard himself say.

"You hardly know her," Bill muttered.

"Are you jealous that someone else is spending time with Noah?" Axel teased.

Bill shrugged and ducked back under the hood of the Prius he was working on.

Axel smiled.

During Hannah's last four days before school started her foster mom had taken the whole family on a special shopping trip and an excursion to the Jersey shore. Hannah had offered to skip the fun so she could watch Noah, but Axel insisted that she join her family.

As a result, Noah had been hanging out at the shop with Axel and Bill all week.

Axel had felt bad letting his apprentice take care of the baby while he talked with customers and did the more difficult jobs himself. But Bill had taken on his new duties cheerfully.

Axel hadn't suspected the transition to having a nanny would be hard on his apprentice. Not that he could blame the man. Noah was a pretty awesome little guy.

The only actual mystery was why Axel had been so

quick and passionate about defending Delilah. Bill was right - he hardly knew her.

He had a sudden memory of her scent, like honeysuckle, and the bear stirred approvingly in his chest.

No way.

He was *not* going to fall for the nanny. Not only because it was classic after-school-special fodder, and also deeply problematic, given the obvious balance of power between them - but because it was just plain wrong for his kid. Noah needed things to be consistent in his world. His dad lusting after the nanny would not make things better.

Keep it professional, champ, he told the bear.

"Whose BMW is that?" he asked Bill.

"The one in the lot?" Bill asked, his head popping up comically.

"Yeah," Axel said, wondering what other BMW he could be talking about. They didn't work on a lot of beamers. Plenty of people in Tarker's Hollow had money, but they weren't usually very ostentatious with it. Ten-year-old Volvos were more the norm.

"I dunno," Bill said.

"Did you check the messages?" Axel asked.

"Yeah, it was just the guy looking for an ETA on the Prius," Bill said. "And the keys for the beamer were in the drop box - no note."

"Damn," Axel said, racking his brain about who might have dropped it off.

The only downside to being a mechanic in a small town was that wherever he went people would pull him aside and ask about their cars.

While it was definitely hilarious to hear them try to imitate odd engine noises, he usually just wound up telling people to drop by and let him have a look.

Most of them didn't, until they needed an oil change or a serious repair.

But once in a while someone just dropped off a car unexpectedly. He was normally around when they dropped off the vehicle. But not this time.

The only recent car conversation he could remember was about a week ago when Dr. Ryan Stevenson had asked if he might be willing to take a look at his grandmother's car, which she was getting ready to sell. Axel had told him to feel free to drop it off and he'd give it a once-over.

He glanced out the window at the BMW. It was a few years old, but it looked spectacular - the paint job was still glistening. It seemed over-the-top for an old lady's car - especially a car she was about to upgrade.

But the Stevensons did have money. Maybe Grandma Stevenson was buying a brand-new BMW. He couldn't fault her for it. They were wonderful machines.

He made a mental note to take a look at it when he was done working on the ancient Saab that was waiting for him in the bay.

He sighed and headed over. Saabs were great cars, but you had to remove half the engine just to change a spark plug. He'd been babying this thing for a family in town for years.

He rolled up his sleeves and popped the hood.

And although he didn't mean for it to happen, he found himself wondering what Delilah was up to, and picturing her holding Noah and looking around her little room.

4

DELILAH

Delilah sat on the floor next to Noah's bedroom door.

She wasn't exactly sure how long naps were supposed to take, but she was pretty sure it wouldn't be good for the baby to wake up alone.

From her cozy spot, she could see down the stairs to the front door. And straight ahead of her, the door to her own room stood open.

My own room...

She'd never really had a room she thought of as her own.

Growing up, she and her mom had moved around almost constantly. And her adult life had her scrambling to get out of dodge at the end of every con.

She knew it wasn't really hers, but there was something so peaceful about the little room with the pretty view. She felt she could stay here happily for quite some time.

If only the real nanny weren't coming soon.

And if she hadn't left the BMW at the shop.

She cursed herself inwardly yet again. Axel seemed like a good man. It wasn't right to have mixed him up in this.

And yet, she wasn't sure what else she could have done.

The con had been a good one - a simple variation on the fiddle game, but played with a flute, since it was the least expensive instrument available at the local pawnshop.

It was supposed to be easy.

Delilah went into the restaurant wearing simple clothing, carrying the flute in a bag, as if she were a subway musician. When her bill came, she was supposed to freak out and say she had forgotten her wallet. Then she would offer to leave her flute, which was her livelihood, as collateral while she ran back to her apartment for her money.

While she was away, a second con artist, pretending to be another diner, would examine the flute and say it was a priceless Verne Q. Powell from the 1939 World's Fair. She would say it was exquisite and that she would pay two hundred thousand dollars for it.

Of course Delilah made sure to have the Powell name engraved on the instrument after purchasing it for twenty-five dollars at the pawn shop, so the suggestion would seem to check out.

The other con artist would say she had to leave for an important appointment, but would leave her card for the flute's owner to call her on her return.

A few minutes after she left, Delilah would return with her wallet.

This was where the mark was supposed to make his move. And the whole con relied on his greed, which is why it always worked.

The mark was supposed to hold onto the card and offer to buy the violin, but for substantially less than the other con artist had said it was worth - thus leaving himself plenty of "profit" when he called the number on the card to resell the instrument.

Then Delilah would take his money and the number on the card would be out of service when he called.

Things did go well, until the point when Delilah returned to the restaurant with her wallet.

The mark offered to buy the violin for a thousand dollars.

She negotiated her way up to two thousand, then accompanied him to an ATM where he tried to withdraw the funds while she hung back, not wanting to be caught on camera.

But he wasn't able to pull out more than a few hundred dollars from the ATM at once and the bank was closed.

He looked downcast for a moment, then brightened.

"I'll give you my car as collateral," he said, pointing to the BMW, which was the reason they'd targeted him in the first place.

It was a few years old, but beautifully kept. They'd figured a guy who drove a car like that would be able to come up with a couple thousand bucks no problem.

"Your car?" she'd asked, still pretending to be a poor street musician.

"Sure," he said. "It's after business hours but we can come back to the bank in the morning. I'll hold onto the flute and you can take the car, for peace of mind."

She thought it out quickly.

No way could she leave the guy alone overnight with the flute without him realizing it was a con. He'd only have to do the tiniest amount of online research to realize he'd been conned.

But the parts alone on the car were worth more than two grand to the fencer her team worked with. She could take the car and be gone before morning.

"Fine," she said.

He gave her the keys.

"Any chance you can give me a ride though?" he asked. "I'm late for my shift."

"Sure," she'd told him.

She'd been horrified when he asked her to drop him off at a chain restaurant where he explained that he worked as a bus boy.

"How did you afford a car like this?" she asked.

"Oh, it's my uncle's, but he lets me drive it sometimes," he said. "See you tomorrow."

She'd sat in the car a long time after dropping him off, then called her partners to tell them she was going to leave the keys on the seat and get out of there.

Delilah knew what she was, and she was not a good person. She stole things for a living.

But she never stole from someone who couldn't afford to be robbed.

And this man clearly couldn't.

If she ditched the job now, they were out less than fifty bucks for the flute and the engraving. It was no big deal.

But when she'd called her partners, they hadn't seen it that way. They told her the two grand was on her, one way or the other. And they weren't the type of people to overlook a debt.

She didn't know what else to do. So she drove away in the BMW.

Only instead of bringing the car to the fence, she kept right on driving.

She hoped that if she ditched the car at an auto shop

that it would be returned to the owner as soon as he reported it stolen.

All she had to do was get on the right side of her partners again. They would be mad, but they would forgive her. She was sure of it. As long as she found some way to make it up to them.

As if on cue, her phone vibrated in her pocket, snapping her back into the present.

She leapt up and padded down the hall to her room, not wanting to wake the baby.

She glanced at the phone before picking up.

THE BARRACUDA

"HEY," she muttered.

"Where the fuck are you?" her partner shrilled. "Where's the car?"

"I'm not giving the car to the fence," Delilah said calmly.

"Just because you went soft doesn't mean you don't owe us our cut," the woman on the other end hissed.

"Us?" Delilah asked. "It was me and you - no one else worked on this."

"Hank helped set up the plan," the woman said.

"*The plan* was the oldest con in the book," Delilah said, allowing her voice to get a little louder. "Hank didn't invent it."

"He found the mark," her partner pointed out.

"Yeah and he didn't do his homework," Delilah said. "The guy's a busboy and that car belongs to his uncle. We're not taking it."

"Newsflash, kid, you already took it," the woman sneered.

"Well, he's getting it back," Delilah said, gritting her teeth.

"I'm putting Hank on," her partner said coldly.

"No, don't do that—" Delilah began.

"You have forty-eight hours to get us our cut," Hank's voice said into the receiver. "I'm not going easy on you. Forty-eight hours, kid, or I will find you, and you will be sorry."

Delilah closed her eyes and leaned against the wall.

She had just put herself on the line to save a busboy who was willing to scam her out of what he thought was a two-hundred-thousand-dollar flute.

"I can't get you the BMW, I don't have it anymore," she admitted. "But I'll find you another car."

"I don't care what you get. Get *something*. I want my cut," the Barracuda yelled in the background.

"Forty-eight hours," Hank repeated and hung up.

Her heart pounded and she looked around, wondering how she had managed to feel so safe here just a few minutes ago.

"Think, Delilah, think, think, think," she whispered to herself, pacing the hallway.

The town looked wealthy enough. Surely there was another quick con she could pull here.

As if on cue, there was a soft cry from Noah's room.

"Hey baby," she called to him. "I'm coming."

She burst into the room, noticing the sweet scent and the colorful alphabet painted painstakingly on the wall even as she rushed to the crib.

Noah's little face was pink and squeezed up.

"Here we are," she cooed instinctively as she considered how best to scoop him up. She knew moms on TV somehow supported the head of a small baby.

He quieted as soon as he saw her leaning over him and blinked up at her with those wide, denim blue eyes.

She found it surprisingly easy to slide her hands under him and tuck him snugly into her chest once again.

He wrapped a chubby fist around a hank of her hair while making a sound that was kind of like a door squeaking open.

"Hi," she replied. "That's better, isn't it?"

He felt heavier than before, his bottom was mushy.

"Oh wow, you have a full diaper," she said, her mind racing. Could it be that different from changing a doll diaper? And when had she last done that?

She saw a changing table in the corner and laid him down carefully.

He launched into a long conversation that mostly sounded like *bababababababbababa* as she struggled with all the tiny snaps on his outfit.

The diaper was only wet, and she thanked her lucky stars that she would learn to change a diaper without poop involved.

"Please don't pee on me," she asked him.

"Babababababa," he replied, and then shoved his small fist into his mouth like a cork, stopping the flow of conversation.

It was the best assurance she was going to get.

Somehow, she managed to get another diaper onto him, and the many tiny snaps snapped properly. Although she was glad she didn't have an audience, because she certainly hadn't looked like the pro she was supposed to be.

"We did it," she crowed as she lifted him up again. "Let's go see your daddy."

If she was being honest, Noah wasn't the only one looking forward to seeing the man again.

5

DELILAH

The walk to the shop was a quick one. Delilah hoped she could find a subtle way to ask about feeding the baby.

She opened the door and the little bell above it jingled merrily.

The place smelled safe and familiar, like the attached garage of her great-grandfather's little house. She remembered a few happy mornings watching him tinker on his car when she had stayed with him as a small child, before her mom took her back out into the whirlwind of a life they shared.

"Hey there," Axel's deep voice boomed.

"Um, hi," Delilah replied. "Noah woke up and we missed you."

Her cheeks flushed.

"That is, *he* missed you," she corrected herself.

A head of curly auburn hair popped up from under the hood of a small gray car. Its owner eyed her suspiciously.

"That was a short nap," he said.

"Bill, this is Delilah, she'll be taking care of Noah," Axel said quickly. "Delilah, this is Bill. He's my apprentice."

"Did you change him when he woke up?" Bill asked.

"Of course," Delilah said.

"Did you feed him?"

"Enough, Bill," Axel chuckled. "Bill helped out with Noah for a few days before you got here, and now he's an expert in all things Noah."

"Actually, I didn't feed him," Delilah admitted.

"I'll take care of it." Bill sighed dramatically and marched into the back room.

"Don't let him bother you," Axel said with a wink. "I think he likes taking care of Noah more than he likes fixing cars."

Delilah smiled back at him, feeling relieved.

He really was handsome. It was hard not to melt just a little in his steel-blue gaze.

"So what are the two of you planning to do this after-noon?" Axel asked, clearing his throat.

"Oh, um, I wasn't sure," she said.

"He likes to go for a walk," Axel suggested. "If you want to take him shopping for whatever you want for dinner that would be amazing."

"Sure," she said.

He dug in his pocket and handed her a wad of bills. "Get whatever you want."

Nice.

"The agency said you were a great cook," Axel contin-ued. "I'm looking forward to it."

Oh crap.

Delilah wasn't a great cook. She wasn't even a good cook.

She honestly couldn't remember the last time she'd operated a stove.

"Let me have him," Bill said as he reentered the room with a blanket and a bottle, saving her from having to respond.

Axel nodded.

Delilah watched intently as Bill sat, draped a blanket over his chest and held out his arms for her to hand Noah to him.

He settled the baby in the crook of his arm and offered him the bottle.

Noah began drinking right away.

So feeding him would be fairly easy. If only she'd been able to watch Bill prepare the formula.

"The stroller's over there if you want to set it up while you're waiting," Axel said, pointing to the corner.

Sure enough, a stroller leaned against the wall of the waiting area.

She could make out the wheels, but the thing was folded up like a piece of origami.

Delilah approached it as if it were a wild animal. She ran a hand down one side and then the other, hoping she didn't look as confused about the way it opened as she felt.

"Here, let me show you," Axel said. "These things are so complicated.

He took a few minutes to show her how to open it up and fold it back.

As she watched, she couldn't help but notice again how handsome he was, muscles flexing with every movement.

And he was nice too - really nice. He could have made her feel bad about not knowing how to open the stroller, but he hadn't.

She figured he must really love Noah to buy him such a complicated stroller. Since he spent his days working on vehicles, it made sense that he would appreciate a good one for his baby.

After one bungled attempt, she was able to repeat the steps pretty easily.

"Thanks," she said.

"Make sure you get yourself a coffee while you're in town," Axel recommended. "There's a great spot - cheesy name, but good coffee - it's called Edible Complex. It's next to the train station."

"Thanks," she said. "Do you have a key to the house for me? I need to lock up before we go."

His eyebrows went up.

"Uh, I think I may have one around," he said. "But honestly I'm not a hundred percent sure they work. I don't really lock the doors except at night."

What an idiot. Who didn't lock their doors?

She tried her best not to look shocked.

"Okay, he's all set," Bill said, saving her yet again from having to reply. "I burped him too, so he should be cheerful for a while."

Noah certainly looked cheerful. He grinned at Delilah and grabbed for her hair again.

"Easy does it, little guy," Axel said, taking him from Bill.

He showed Delilah how to strap the baby in. There was a cozy built-in sleeping bag looking thing to keep Noah warm, and there were straps to keep him safe.

"Hey, do we need to return this to Joe Crow?" Bill yelled to Axel.

He was pointing in the direction of a beautifully restored classic Mustang. The paint was so glossy it looked wet.

"Nah, there's no rush," Axel said. "He's got like ten of those in his garage - he won't miss it."

Delilah's mouth dropped open.

A mint-condition Mustang like that was probably worth thirty thousand dollars or more.

Someone in this town had *ten* of them in his garage, and *wouldn't miss one*?

"Delilah, if you need anything at all while you're in town you can just tell the store employee you're Noah's caregiver and they'll let you use the phone," Axel said, handing her a business card with the shop's number on it.

"Thanks," she said breathlessly. "Are you ready, Noah?"

Noah made a happy yelping noise.

"I guess that's our cue," she said.

Axel opened the door for them, and she pushed the stroller out into the sunlight.

The gravel parking area was a little bumpy, but the stroller was well-built, and Noah didn't complain.

She managed to make it out of sight of the shop before she reached for her phone and thumbed the contact for the Barracuda.

She picked up on the first ring.

"I've got something for you," Delilah said. "A restored classic Mustang."

"Sounds old," the woman said dubiously.

"It is," Delilah said. "Probably a sixty-seven or sixty-eight, which means in this condition it's worth way more than that used BMW."

"Where is it?" her partner demanded immediately.

Delilah gave her the address and explained the situation. Leaving out the parts about how her room made her feel like she was home, and Axel's smile made her feel like she might not ever leave.

"*You're* working as his nanny?" the woman asked derisively.

"Only for a couple of days," Delilah said, looking at the

top of Noah's downy head and wondering if she didn't wish it was for longer. "It's actually going pretty well. The baby's really nice."

But the Barracuda had already hung up. She'd never really been the maternal type.

6

DELILAH

Delilah wandered the aisles of the Co-op grocery store in downtown Tarker's Hollow, wondering how she would ever manage to even buy the right ingredients, let alone cook dinner.

Every grocery store she had ever visited before this had a section with magazines. On her way here she'd convinced herself that one of the magazines would have an easy recipe. Then all she'd have to do was buy it and the ingredient list and she'd be all set.

But this place was like no grocery store she'd ever seen.

There were bouquets of flowers from nearby gardens, racks of handmade soaps and lip balms, and even a section of woolen hats and mittens made by women in developing countries.

There were no magazines.

There were no TV dinners, which had been her back-up plan.

There was a whole wall of bins of nuts and spices, and there were foods she'd never even heard of.

The section with the meats was patrolled by a pair of

actual butchers in white aprons, who seemed to engage every customer in their section in a conversation about what they were cooking.

She wondered briefly if maybe they could suggest something easy to cook.

But there were too many people everywhere. What if someone here knew Axel and told him what she'd been up to?

As if on cue, an older woman with dark hair in a bun approached. "Noah," she sang out, smiling at the baby.

Noah grinned back at her and kicked his legs inside his little blanket bag.

"You must be the new nanny," the lady said. "I'm Eva Cortez."

"I'm Delilah," she replied. "Nice to meet you."

"So you're out shopping?" Eva asked. "Axel's a lucky man to have a nanny who can cook."

Eva looked so friendly and her eyes were so kind...

"I was just wondering what to fix him," Delilah admitted. "It's my first day."

"Well, you know he loves the meatloaf from the little restaurant across the street, All Occasions," Eva confided. "Maybe you could try your own take on it."

"Great idea," Delilah said. "I'll head over and try a piece, so I know what he likes."

"Well, welcome to town," Eva said. "I hope to see you again soon."

Delilah gave Eva a little wave and scurried away before she could mess up what had seemed like a pleasant conversation.

She took the stroller past the Co-op's patio of picnic benches with umbrellas where a group of moms sat with their own strollers.

Sure enough, there was a tiny restaurant across the street with a sign that said *All Occasions*.

She headed over and stood in front of the door trying to figure out how she was supposed to get in.

There was an automatic door at the Co-op. But this was just a simple glass door with a handle.

She could reach the handle or push the stroller, not both.

But before she could solve the puzzle, an elderly gentleman inside opened the door.

"Thank you," she said.

"My pleasure, dear," said the man. "And hello to you, Mr. Noah."

Noah squeaked back at him and the man smiled so hard his eyes almost disappeared.

"Are you here for the meatloaf?" the pretty lady behind the counter asked knowingly.

"It's Axel's favorite, right?" Delilah asked.

"Sure is," the lady replied. "I'll box up enough for both of you."

"I don't suppose you'd want to share the recipe?" Delilah asked, figuring it couldn't hurt.

"Oh, that particular recipe is my livelihood," the woman laughed. "But I hear there's a very nice meatloaf recipe on the HomeAtLast website. Lots of good amateur cooking tips there. Not that you need it. Axel has been bragging that his new nanny was an excellent cook."

"Wow, word travels fast," Delilah said, wondering where the heck she was supposed to get her hands on a recipe when everyone in this town apparently already thought she was Gordon flipping Ramsay.

"Sure does," the lady agreed. "We don't have much else to talk about. Hang on while I get your meal. It'll be about ten minutes, if there's anything else you need to get done around town."

"Oh, maybe I'll get a coffee at Edible Complex," Delilah said, remembering Axel's suggestion.

"Great cappuccino there," the lady said, nodding.

Delilah headed for the door where the older man was already waiting for her.

"Thank you so much," Delilah enthused as he opened the door for them.

She couldn't believe her own cheery behavior.

The little town must be rubbing off on her.

She and Noah headed down the half block toward the little brick Victorian train station.

"Hey, Noah," called a lady who was sweeping the sidewalk in front of a little real estate office.

Delilah smiled at her.

"Beautiful day," said a man, coming down the sidewalk in the opposite direction. He actually tipped his hat, like he was on TV or something.

Delilah nodded and kept walking, feeling like she was on the set of some holiday movie.

At last she reached the café. There was a sign on it that identified it as *Edible Complex*.

A mom with a stroller was just going in as she arrived, and Delilah studied the woman's backwards door opening technique and copied it when she entered.

The café was larger than it looked from outside. The delicious scents of coffee and fresh cooked bacon dueled for her attention.

The walls were hung with original paintings and framed photographs, all of which had plaques with the artist's name and a price underneath.

Delilah got in line and looked around at the other patrons.

There were tons of college students working on tablets and laptops. She had almost forgotten this was a college town.

Their relaxed enjoyment made her wonder what it would have been like to go to college herself. Her education had been markedly different.

A couple of women with strollers sat in a sunny corner, eating breakfast.

A man working on a laptop got up and headed to the door with a *Unisex Bathroom* sign above it.

He just left the laptop right on the table.

Delilah glanced at the screen.

The computer was open and logged in.

Idiot.

She waited for someone to swoop in and snatch the computer.

But no one even looked up.

"What can I get for you?" the barista asked.

The line had cleared without her even noticing.

Delilah blinked at the man. He looked to be in his twenties, with a beret and a handlebar mustache.

"Uh, cappuccino, please," she managed, handing him a ten.

"Sure thing," he said, making change for her.

She glanced back at the laptop.

It was still there.

"Here you go," the barista told her, handing her some change. "Coffee will be over there as soon as we're done making it."

She slid the change into her pocket and headed to the other end of the counter to wait.

To her amazement, the laptop was still open on the table.

What kind of person just did that? Didn't he know what was going to happen?

But the man came out of the bathroom, sat down and began to type again.

"Cappuccino's up," the barista sang out.

Delilah grabbed her coffee and headed back out to All Occasions.

A little dress shop on the way had racks of beautiful dresses on display out on the sidewalk.

There was not an employee in sight anywhere.

A car pulled up in front of the dress shop and a man jumped out.

Here we go, Delilah thought to herself.

But the man didn't take the dresses.

He left his car keys on the dash of the car and sprinted to the dry cleaner's shop across the street.

The windows of the car were open.

Delilah looked at the car for a moment and allowed herself to imagine just jumping in and driving the car away.

"*Stop,*" someone cried.

She spun around, feeling guilty even though she hadn't acted on her urges.

The barista from Edible Complex was jogging toward her, handlebars of his mustache bouncing jauntily.

"I'm so sorry," he said. "You gave me a ten and I only gave you change for a five."

Sheesh. She'd been so busy worrying about the guy's laptop she hadn't even noticed being shorted her own change.

"Thanks," she said, accepting the bills.

The barista nodded and headed back to the café.

Delilah stood for just a moment, looking around the little town with the tall trees and the friendly people.

She figured it probably made sense to stick around as long as she could. This town was ripe for the picking.

But something deep inside her, a voice she hadn't heard in a long time, was wondering what it would be like to live someplace where she didn't have to look over her shoulder all the time.

Where she could walk away from her car or laptop and expect it to still be there when she returned.

Where she didn't have to lock her doors.

7

AXEL

Axel found himself eager to close up the shop and head home.

He whistled as he turned off the lights and locked the garage bays.

"Someone's got a spring in his step," Bill teased. "I guess you can't wait to get home to that hot nanny."

"She's not hot," Axel snapped defensively.

But she was hot, and they both knew it.

He tried not to picture her curvy body and those big, dark eyes.

"Uh, she's hot, dude, wake up," Bill said. "Doesn't mean she's a good nanny though. Keep an eye on her. She's basically a stranger."

"Yeah, yeah," Axel said. "Noah likes her. I've got a good feeling about it."

"See you tomorrow," Bill said, rolling his eyes.

The short walk from the shop back to the house seemed to stretch out to an eternity. Axel found himself appreciating the sunset over the trees and the warm light in the downstairs windows.

A delicious scent greeted him as soon as he opened the front door.

Then he heard the singing.

Delilah was crooning a Beatles song in a soft contralto while Noah growled and squeaked along delightedly.

Axel closed his eyes, struck by a pang of longing he couldn't explain.

His inner bear nosed at the boundaries, intrigued by the good smells and happy sounds.

"Axel?" Delilah's worried voice cut through the fog.

"Hey," he said, heading into the kitchen.

Her smile of relief was like a rainbow after a storm.

"Sorry," she said. "I guess I'm just not used to leaving doors unlocked."

"You don't have to," he told her quickly. "If you guys don't feel safe, I'll make sure we have keys tomorrow."

"I know you're right there at the shop," she said. "Don't worry about it."

His bear preened at her assertion that his presence meant she was safe.

But Axel vowed to himself that he'd get the key situation straightened out in the morning anyway. He wanted Delilah to feel at home here.

"It's kind of a sleepy town," he explained. "And I don't know why, but I just don't worry about anyone breaking in."

"I know why," she said, giving his big body an appreciative once-over.

He tried not to grin and failed.

If she only knew.

"Anyway, I'll make sure to get you a key," he said. "And you can always lock the door if you're here alone with Noah. I'll ring the bell if I need to come in and I don't have a key."

"Everyone here is so trusting," Delilah observed.

"We're pretty lucky to live in a small, tight-knit community," Axel said. "Not too much happens around here."

What he had said wasn't quite true for the shifters of Tarker's Hollow, who had enjoyed a rather adventurous few years.

But as far as the humans in Tarker's Hollow were concerned, it was completely accurate. And since most of the town was made up of humans, he figured it was a fair statement.

"Something smells amazing," he said.

"Oh, the meatloaf," she cried and grabbed a kitchen towel.

"My favorite," he said, feeling surprised but very pleased.

He watched as she bent to pull a pan out of the oven.

"It's okay," she breathed in relief as she pulled out a steaming platter.

Noah chuckled from the doorway and banged on the tray of his jumperoo.

Axel scooped him up and gave him a cuddle, inhaling the sweet scent of him.

"Were you a good boy today?" he asked him between kisses.

"He was a great boy today," Delilah said. "But I'll bet he's getting hungry. I'll get him a bottle fixed when I'm done with dinner."

"I'll get it," Axel said.

He tucked the baby onto his hip and pulled out the formula and a clean bottle.

Delilah had turned around to watch him.

Maybe she thought he couldn't fix a bottle because he was a guy. Plenty of women seemed to think it was a miracle he could keep Noah alive on his own.

Well if she thought she was going to find fault with his parenting, she was mistaken. Axel was a great dad, and he made every effort to keep his son well fed and his bottles properly sanitized.

He went through the whole process methodically as she watched him closely, mixing the formula, warming the bottle.

At last he snuggled Noah in close and offered him his meal.

The baby tucked into his dinner enthusiastically.

"I know I don't have a degree in early childhood education, but I can fix his bottle," Axel said, looking down at his son who was wolfing down the milk happily.

"Oh," she said. "I didn't mean to stare. I just... I haven't seen many dads preparing bottles, that's all."

He looked up at her.

Her dark eyes were stricken.

The bear could scent her shame.

She was telling the truth.

"Sorry," he said. "I guess I have a bit of a chip on my shoulder. The moms at Noah's playgroup always look at me like I'm about to drop him or something."

"Noah is in a *playgroup*?" she asked.

"Well, he doesn't really play," he said. "At least not yet. Some of the toddlers play together. But for the parents of the infants, it's more of a place for us to hang out."

"I see," she said, nodding and opening a cabinet.

"I'm friends with a couple of other single dads and caregivers," he went on. "And the moms don't exactly welcome us with open arms."

"That sucks," Delilah said, placing two plates on the counter. "Oh. Sorry about my language."

"He's heard worse," Axel laughed. "But thanks. Hey, you're pretty easy to talk to. You know that?"

She smiled and looked down at the plates.

There was something about her, something so vulnerable in spite of her air of independence.

Mine, his bear said softly.

Axel nearly gasped.

Down boy.

Surely this woman couldn't be his mate. He had just met her.

Mine.

8

DELILAH

Delilah smiled back at Axel, wondering why she felt so connected to him.

He's the mark, she reminded herself. *You can't go falling in lust with him.*

But it wasn't lust.

Well, it wasn't *just* lust. True, his big body drew her in like a magnet. But there was something deeper between them. Something stronger that pulled and ripped at her heart.

And that didn't make any sense.

Noah spat the bottle out and began to cry.

"Oh, buddy, you need to burp, don't you?" Axel crooned.

He held the baby against his shoulder and rubbed between his tiny shoulder blades.

There was silence for a moment and then a burp so gigantic it seemed impossible that it could have been contained in such a tiny package.

"Wow," Delilah murmured.

"Yeah, he's a good burper," Axel said.

She had to smile at the pride in his voice.

But a second later Noah began wailing again.

"It's okay, buddy, I've got you," Axel told him, rubbing that tiny back again.

But Noah didn't burp. He just screamed louder. His whole little face went red.

"What's wrong?" Delilah asked, feeling a little frantic.

"He can be a little colicky," Axel told her. "Sometimes I just walk with him for a while until he falls asleep."

"Oh," Delilah said, stunned that a cry like that could be solved by walking.

"I'm really sorry about dinner," Axel said. "You don't have to wait for me. Go ahead and enjoy yours while it's warm."

She realized he had misunderstood her dismay.

"Oh no, I don't care about dinner," she said. "Why don't I help with the baby?"

"You don't have to do that," Axel said. "It's after hours."

"I want to learn to comfort him," Delilah said. "And he should know I'm here for him."

"Okay," he told her with another warm smile. "I'll just be pacing with him. Want to come out on the back porch with us?"

She nodded and followed him to the back door.

The covered porch had a painted blue floor and finished wood ceiling that made it feel cozy in spite of the sweeping view over the wooded hillside behind the small fenced backyard.

The sky had gone pink with cotton candy clouds over the dark trees.

"It's so beautiful out here," she breathed.

"Yeah," he said. "I never get used to it. I honestly would have bought the house no matter what, since it's behind the garage, but this really sold me."

Noah's cries grew louder again.

"Oh boy, you're feeling rough, aren't you, little man?" Axel said to the baby, cradling Noah's silken head in his big hand.

"He likes singing," Delilah heard herself say.

Axel turned to her. "Do you want to take him for a minute?"

She opened her arms.

Noah's warmth filled her heart, she didn't care that he was screaming his head off.

"Hi, baby," she murmured.

He wrenched himself around in her arms with a strength she didn't know he had.

Delilah hung onto him for dear life, hoping she wasn't hurting him.

"*Hush little baby, don't say a word, Daddy's gonna buy you a mockingbird*," she sang softly.

Noah froze for a moment, then began crying again.

"*If that mockingbird don't sing, Daddy's gonna buy you a diamond ring*," she went on.

Noah's cries dampened to whimpers.

"Walk with him a little," Axel whispered to her.

"*If that diamond ring turns brass, Daddy's gonna buy you a looking glass*," she sang, walking carefully down the length of the porch.

It was easier to hold him now that he wasn't squirming. She felt her heart rate slow as she sang on.

The last rays of sunlight licked their flames over the trees as the sky deepened to velvet blue. The night birds and cicadas began to join Delilah's song.

Noah stopped whimpering and tucked his little face into the crook of her neck as she sang on about all the things his father would bribe him with.

She let her voice get softer.

Noah interrupted the song with a reproachful sniff here and there.

At last his warm body softened against her chest as he fell asleep.

She finished the song, enjoying his soft breath and the warm weight of him.

"Holy cow," Axel said. "When he's in a mood like that it usually takes me at least fifteen minutes to calm him down."

"I got lucky," Delilah whispered.

But pride bubbled in her chest. It felt good to have comforted another person, even a miniature one, enough that he would go to sleep right in her arms.

He doesn't know what you are.

She shook her head as if that could rid her of the thought.

"We should get him to bed," Axel said.

She nodded and they headed back inside, through the house and up the stairs to Noah's room.

Axel opened the door and she tiptoed in after him with Noah.

The mattress of the crib suddenly looked so low, and her armful of Noah so high. How in the world was she supposed to get him all the way down there without waking him up?

"I'll help," Axel whispered.

She let him slide Noah out of her arms and rest him gently into his crib.

Noah's lower lip pouted out and his forehead scrunched up, but he didn't open his eyes.

Axel rubbed his little belly gently for a moment and the baby relaxed into a deep sleep.

They stood there a few more minutes, gazing down at the sleeping baby.

Delilah felt a peace so strong it brought tears to her eyes.

"I'll, um, reheat our dinner," she mumbled and fled the room.

She took the steps quickly but quietly, her tears blurring her path as she hurried to the kitchen.

The meatloaf was still steaming.

She took a deep breath and forced herself to survey her handiwork.

The meal had been prepared by the little restaurant, so the meatloaf was already sliced. She had simply dumped a bunch of ketchup on top and stuck it in the oven so it would look different.

She set slices onto their plates quickly, so Axel might not notice that it wasn't a whole meatloaf.

Then she spooned on the vegetables, which she prayed wouldn't be too familiar. She hadn't had time to put cheese on top or do anything to disguise them.

She was setting the plates on the kitchen table when Axel returned.

"Thanks for helping with him," he said softly. "He really likes you."

"I really like him," she replied, feeling heat rush to her cheeks.

"Yeah, he's pretty likable," Axel said, grabbing two water bottles from the refrigerator. "But I may be just a little bit biased."

"If you're not, who will be?" Delilah asked.

She knew the answer to that. When your own parents didn't believe in you, nobody else would either. She'd learned that much from experience.

"I guess you're wondering about his mom," Axel said softly.

"You don't have to tell me anything," Delilah said quickly. "You're a great dad - end of story."

"She was my girlfriend," he told her as he sat down at the table. "We weren't all that serious. But when she got pregnant, I told her right away that I wanted to marry her."

"Wow," Delilah said, wondering how many men would have the same immediate reaction.

She sat opposite him and took the water he offered.

The table was so tiny their knees were practically touching.

"Things weren't perfect with us, but I always wanted a family," he said. "I knew we could make it work if we both wanted to."

Delilah nodded.

"Anyway, she said she wanted to see how things went," he said. "She told me she didn't want us to be married because we felt some obligation. So I agreed. But as the pregnancy went along things got worse and worse. She seemed so restless."

He looked out the window, as if the moonlit view over the porch would help him find the words.

"Anyway, I figured she was tired and that things would be better after the baby was born," he went on. "I felt a lot of sympathy for what we were putting her body through."

Delilah nodded. She had never been pregnant, but the idea of growing a human inside yourself while continuing with all the tasks of daily life seemed impossible.

"The night Noah was born I was so happy," he said. "He was so healthy, so beautiful. I was in awe - I felt so lucky to be his dad."

He took a deep breath and gazed at Delilah, as if gauging her reaction so far.

"But she didn't feel the same," he said. "I fell asleep in

the hospital chair with the baby on my chest. When I woke up, she was gone. She left a note saying it wasn't going to work out. She didn't want to be a mom."

"Oh my God," Delilah breathed.

"I thought maybe it was postpartum depression," he said. "It's very common, and it's dangerous to new moms. I called and texted but she never picked up. I even called the police, worried that she might hurt herself. And, of course, I brought Noah home when they released him."

"Wow," Delilah said.

"I hoped she would be home soon after. It didn't occur to me that she really wasn't coming back until I got a letter from a lawyer a month later," he said. "She was voluntarily relinquishing her parental rights."

"You must have been furious," Delilah said. She was furious herself at anyone who could leave the sweet baby.

"At first I was mad, on Noah's behalf," Axel admitted. "But now I think about it from her point of view. She never wanted a baby. And I wanted a family so much. She had him for me. I didn't realize it at the time, but the pregnancy, the birth, all of that was a sacrifice she made for Noah and for me. And I can't be anything but grateful to her for that."

His blue eyes glistened with emotion.

Delilah had never met a man like this - a man so prone to forgiveness, so dedicated to his small family.

"Anyway, I just thought you should know," he said. "Can't have you hearing the rumors going around town and not knowing the truth."

"Rumors?" she asked.

"I shouldn't say rumors," he said. "Really it's more that everyone seems to feel sorry for me. But I'm happy. Noah is all the family I'll ever need."

She nodded.

He took a big bite of meatloaf.

"Oh wow, this is amazing," he said. "You're an amazing cook. Was this hard to make?"

"Not really," she said, hoping he wouldn't ask a lot of follow-up questions about the recipe. "So Noah's your only family? Do you have anyone else local?"

"Not local. I've got a brother in Glacier City," he said. "But yeah, Noah's it for me here, and he's plenty."

She nodded. Noah would be enough for her too. Noah was lovely and babies were a lot of work - she could see that much already.

"That's enough about me," he said, with a smile. "Probably more than you wanted to hear. Tell me about your family. I want to know all about you, Delilah."

She froze for a moment, feeling like a deer in the headlights.

She couldn't tell him the truth.

But for the first time ever, she couldn't bear to lie either.

He was watching her patiently, the expression on his handsome face telling her plainly that he wasn't just making polite conversation. He wanted to know her.

And there was the pull again, the electric sizzle between them deeper now, inspiring an agony of need that seemed to take hold of her whole body.

Instead of answering, she leaned across the table and kissed him.

9

AXEL

Axel's world seemed to tilt on its axis as Delilah's soft lips pressed against his.

The bear roared in his chest, desperate to claim her, even as his heart ached with the sweetness of her gesture.

She began to pull away and he instinctively cupped her cheek in his hand to stay her, thumbing her jaw open to taste her.

Her tiny moan set his senses on fire. He was glad the table was between them to slow him down.

She kissed him back with such passion. It was as if she could sense his need, as if she knew the bear was beneath the surface, yearning for her.

"Delilah," he murmured, pulling back.

"I-I'm sorry," she said.

She was sorry.

Guilt shot through him. She hadn't meant to kiss him. He had read her responses all wrong. She was his employee. Noah liked her. And he was letting his bear take control.

He got up from the table.

"I'm sorry too, Delilah, I don't know what I was thinking," he said, clearing his plate. "I didn't mean to force myself on you. I hope we can both forget that happened. I'll take care of the kitchen. You go on and relax."

"It's fine," she said, her voice smoother now. "It never happened. We'll clean up together."

He wanted to beg her to leave him. His body was still pounding with desire for her.

But he couldn't bear the idea of sending her away, even just out of the room.

How are you already in my heart?

He nodded and worked on wrapping up the leftovers.

That meatloaf was sensational, and there was enough for him to have a cold sandwich for lunch tomorrow.

He placed the container in the fridge and moved on to the sink, then began to wash the dishes as Delilah wiped the table.

The warm soapy water was pleasant, and he enjoyed the sounds of the chairs being pushed in and out as Delilah worked. It was nice to have another grown-up around.

You'd better remember that and keep your paws off her if you want to keep her here, he reminded his bear sternly.

After a moment, the sounds behind him stopped. There was nothing but the cicada song outside and the gentle rush of running water in the sink.

And then two hands slid around his waist as Delilah rested her head against his back.

He froze, his heart pounding, breath held in anticipation.

"You didn't force yourself on me," she murmured.

He felt her lips press against his shoulder as her hands roved over his abs.

"Delilah," he groaned.

"Shhh," she whispered.

One delicate hand wandered lower, too close to where his raging cock pressed at the fly of his jeans.

He spun around, held her by the shoulders.

"You're playing with fire, Delilah," he warned her.

She gazed up at him with those beautiful dark eyes, her cheeks rosy, and then went up on her toes to kiss him.

There were a million reasons why he knew he shouldn't kiss her back.

But he couldn't seem to remember any of them.

Mine.

He swung her up into his arms and carried her through the dining room and living room and up the stairs to his bedroom.

She wrapped her arms around his neck, pressing herself closer.

He closed the door behind them and turned on a bedside lamp so he could see her.

The bear paced and roared, craving a quick claiming.

Axel fought him back.

"Axel," she moaned as he placed her down gently.

"Is this what you want?" he asked, his voice rough with wanting.

"Yes," she said. "Please, I need you."

Fuck.

All his control was out the window now.

He slid his hands down her sides, loving the soft feel of her, the generous curves that filled his palms.

But when he began to slide her t-shirt up, she stiffened.

"Delilah?" he whispered.

"C-can we turn the light off?" she asked.

"No," he told her. "I need to see you."

"I'm not what you're used to," she told him.

"How the hell would you know what I'm used to?" he asked.

"I'm not thin," she corrected herself.

His heart almost broke.

"You're beautiful," he told her. "You're beautiful and I want to see you."

She didn't reply, but she lifted her arms to make it easier for him to slip the shirt off.

He gasped when he saw her.

She was exquisite. Her luscious breasts nearly bursting out of a lacy bra, her round, soft belly begging to be kissed, her hips wide like the full moon, making him want to howl...

But she had turned away from him, as if he were going to strike her.

Is this how she had been taught to think of her magical body? That it was worthy of punishment?

A woman like this should be worshipped.

But words weren't going to take that hurt away from her.

He was going to show her how to feel.

Fighting every instinct to rush, he slid her jeans down to her ankles and helped her step out.

"Get in bed," he told her.

She crawled in obediently, driving him wild with the sight of her round bottom presented for him in a pair of tiny lace panties.

The bear inside him growled with pleasure at her submission.

When she lay before him, dark hair splayed out on the pillow, he peeled off his own t-shirt.

She gazed at him, lips slightly parted as if the sight of him made her mouth water.

He crawled on top of her and kissed her sweet lips again.

She lifted herself up to meet him and the feel of her warm curves against him sent his blood boiling.

He pulled away and looked into her eyes.

"Be still for me," he warned her. "You're so beautiful, I need to taste my fill."

She blinked, her eyes gone hazy with need.

His cock throbbed in response and he kissed her again, passionately, praying to regain control.

When he broke away, she gasped for breath.

He kissed her forehead, then moved down to nuzzle her neck, teasing himself with the scent of her and the feel of that tender skin his bear desperately wanted him to bite.

It would be so easy. She was so warm and willing, so weak with lust. All he had to do was sink his teeth into her and she would be his forever.

He let his teeth graze her skin as he kissed her, teasing himself.

She moaned gently and arched her back, maddening him with the press of her breasts against his chest.

Somehow, he managed to pull himself away. He ran a trail of kisses down her collarbone, then pulled back to pluck open the front clasp of her bra and release her breasts.

Delilah seemed to hold her breath.

He feasted his eyes on her beautiful breasts and their crinkled brown nipples, stiff and begging for his touch.

He nuzzled them, smiled against her chest when she gasped at the feel of his rough jaw against her tender flesh.

She moaned in earnest when he licked one nipple into his mouth and teased the other with the pad of his thumb.

But when her hips began to quiver, he knew she needed more.

The bear slavered at the scent of her.

Axel needed to taste her more than he needed his next breath.

10

DELILAH

Delilah fought the urge to hide as Axel nuzzled her belly.

She had always been soft and rounded where other women were hard and narrow.

It felt strange to have a man so hungry to see her, so clearly enjoying rubbing his sexy rough cheeks against her tummy.

But he didn't stay there long.

She held her breath as he nudged her thighs apart.

The sensation of his tongue against her almost sent her immediately over the edge.

She clutched the sheets and fought to stay quiet.

He licked her again, a long slow caress.

Delilah moaned.

She felt him smile against her inner thigh as he fed on her wildly, lapping and sucking gently, driving her insane.

The world around her had long since disappeared - even the room was fading. There was only her aching, hungry sex and his wicked mouth.

At last he slid a finger against her opening and flicked her swollen clitoris with his clever tongue.

Delilah cried out brokenly and lost herself in the throes of a pleasure so intense, that it felt almost dangerous.

When he crawled up to hold her, she wrapped her arms around his neck, and her thighs around his hips. She kissed him with abandon, not caring that she could taste herself on his lips.

This couldn't be love - not yet.

But it felt like what she imagined love would feel like - the wordless vulnerability, the need to feel him close.

She slid a hand down the delicious ridges of his abs, eager to taste him too.

But he held her hand and lay beside her instead.

"Axel," she said.

"Let me hold you," he whispered. "I just want to feel you close."

She wanted to argue, but the warmth of his big body was already making her sleepy. And he was sliding his fingers slowly through her hair in long, mesmerizing strokes.

Maybe she would just close her eyes for a second.

She awoke a few hours later.

Axel was restless in his sleep, moaning and tossing.

A shaft of moonlight came through the window, illuminating his muscular form.

He wasn't used to having someone else in his bed. That much was clear.

She sat up and slid out of bed as quietly as she could. No point destroying his rest, fitful as it was.

She grabbed her clothes from the floor and padded out of his room to slip them on in the hallway.

But somehow, she didn't feel like going back to her own bed alone.

Instead, she wandered down to the first floor, and out onto the back porch.

The night air was cool and crisp, and the white fence around the little backyard almost glowed in the moonlight, as if the house were encircled in some sort of magical protection.

She curled up on one of the wicker sofas and pulled a throw blanket around herself.

It was pleasant out here, pleasant enough that it put an ache in the back of her throat.

Change is the only constant, her mother used to say cheerfully as they packed up their lives again and again.

The words never made Delilah's heart any lighter, but they rang true.

She was only going to be here for a few days, so it didn't matter if Noah melted her heart, or Axel melted her body, or if their house felt like a home. Delilah would be moving on.

And maybe that was for the best. Trusting people had never really worked out for her.

And this man was far too easy to trust.

He'd be a great con man, she thought bitterly to herself.

But she couldn't bring herself to really believe it. Axel was one in a million - a genuine man.

It didn't matter anyway - she was helping her partners steal one of his customer's cars.

And though he surely had insurance for that sort of thing, and it sounded like the customer would hardly be bothered, she knew Axel would be horrified when he found the car was gone.

You're leaving when they take the car, she reminded herself. *You won't have to see his reaction.*

The idea of it felt like breaking herself into pieces but it would actually be kinder to herself to remember things this way - peaceful and pleasant.

Assuming he could look her in the eye in the morning. The night had been fun. For her at least. But then he'd pulled away.

Why wouldn't he let me touch him?

Delilah couldn't make heads or tails of it. In her experience, most guys were only out for their own pleasure - especially when they fooled around with the babysitter, which, like it or not, was the best way to describe what had happened last night.

In the moment it had felt like love. Or at least like passion.

But now, in the cool air of the night, Delilah had to be honest with herself. It wasn't likely that tonight had meant anything to him at all.

When Axel woke up, he might be pissed at her for kissing him. Or he might pretend it never happened.

Or he might fire her.

Shit.

If he fired her, she would lose access to the car.

She willed herself not to think about it.

The best thing she could do was pretend the whole thing never happened. If she ignored it first, he could just relax and know that all was well.

The chirping of the cicadas picked up again and she breathed in the damp, fresh air and closed her eyes to lose herself in their lullaby.

11

AXEL

Axel awoke feeling happy.

In his dim half-wakefulness, his bear rejoiced, and he reached across the bed for his mate, then moaned in disappointment when he realized he was alone.

Axel blinked into consciousness and promptly remembered everything.

"Delilah," he murmured.

He closed his eyes again and pictured her mischievous smile as he teased her, and her soft cries when he finally gave her what she wanted.

Why did she leave?

He remembered holding her as she fell asleep.

Maybe the baby woke up.

But a quick check of the monitor showed him the grainy picture of Noah still sleeping in his crib, legs frogged out and eyelashes kissing his chubby cheeks.

Axel rolled out of bed and grabbed a fresh set of clothes. He figured he'd better shower and get ready for the day before tracking her down. Noah had a doctor's appointment pretty early.

He grabbed the monitor and headed into the bathroom.

The hot water from the shower felt heavenly. He was tempted to let off a little steam from his encounter with Delilah last night.

But somehow it didn't appeal.

He was beginning to worry that he had made a big mistake, that he'd moved way too fast and scared her.

He finished his shower and dressed quickly.

The door to her room was empty, and her bed was made. She must be up.

Maybe she had spent the whole night with him and just gotten up a bit earlier.

He headed downstairs with a spring in his step.

But she wasn't downstairs either.

A terrible thought occurred to him and he ran to the front door.

She was nowhere in sight.

If she had chosen to follow the gravel path back up to the street and out of their lives, he was too late to stop her.

Axel, what have you done?

But he knew what he had done. He had allowed himself to be selfish and he had driven another woman out of his life.

The sound of Noah stirring on the monitor was a relief.

He jogged upstairs and swept the baby up before he could fully awaken.

"Just you and me, bud," he whispered into that sweet, downy head.

Noah banged his little forehead against Axel's chest.

"Yes, yes, I know you're hungry," Axel said. "Come on, little bear. I'll make you a bottle."

They headed down to the kitchen and Axel started warming a bottle.

The sunrise over the trees called to him and he stepped onto the back porch to wait for the bottle to warm.

Her scent called to his bear, warm and sweet.

She was curled up on one of his wicker sofas under a blanket, sleeping.

The early morning light played on the highlights in her dark hair and her mouth was curved up slightly, like she was having a happy dream.

He wished he and Noah could step into that dream with her.

"Bah," said Noah suddenly.

Delilah blinked and began to stretch under the blanket.

"Sorry we woke you," Axel said softly. "I'm really glad you're here."

Her dark eyes fixed on his for a moment, then she smiled.

"Bah," Noah said again, thrusting his arms out to Delilah to be held.

"No, no, Delilah just woke up," Axel told him.

"He's fine," Delilah said fondly, holding out her arms.

Axel handed over his son and watch her cuddle him close. Noah settled right in, snuggling his face into the crook of her neck. The two of them curled up in the blanket was the coziest thing Axel had ever seen.

A ding from the kitchen told him the bottle was ready.

"Go ahead," Delilah said. "We'll be here."

He headed for the kitchen, humming merrily as he prepared the day's first bottle.

"Here we go," Axel said.

Delilah held her hand out for the bottle and he watched her offer it to his son.

For a long time, they were quiet. The birdsong and

Noah's noisy enjoyment of his meal made their silence cheerful.

"He has a checkup at the pediatrician's this morning," Axel heard himself say at last. "Want to come?"

"Yes," Delilah said quickly. "I'd love to."

She glanced down at her clothes. The same ones she'd been wearing when she arrived.

"I guess I don't really have anything to wear," she admitted.

"Oh yeah. Sorry," he said, feeling guilty for not finding something more comfortable for her to sleep in. "I still have a few things in the hall closet from Hannah, Noah's summertime sitter. She learned pretty quickly that having a change of clothes handy was never a bad idea when you were minding a baby. They should work for now, and after Noah's appointment, we can stop at one of the shops in town and get you a few things to hold you over until you get your luggage back."

"That sounds nice," she said with a sweet smile.

And just like that, he knew things were fine between them.

Better than fine.

When Noah was finished with his meal, Axel took him up to get ready while Delilah found the change of clothes and took a shower.

They headed out a few minutes later in Axel's station wagon. He'd bought it used from a customer when it became clear that his other car wasn't practical for securing a car seat.

Delilah sat beside him, gazing out the window with a dreamy expression.

Though he badly wanted to know what she was thinking, he was loath to break the spell and kept his eyes on the road as best he could until they had parked at the hospital.

Noah's doctor had a practice on the second floor of the annex, but there was free parking in the main hospital garage.

They got out, unstrapped Noah and headed inside.

"This place is huge," Delilah remarked.

"There's a fitness center here and plenty of doctors who use the building for daily practice," Axel explained.

"Axel," someone called to him from the elevator.

"Hey, Dr. Stevenson," Axel said.

"You know it's just Ryan to you," the man replied with a twinkle in his eye.

"Hey, I got the car," Axel said, remembering. "I'll call you as soon as I've checked it out."

"What car?" Ryan asked.

"Maybe your grandmother dropped it off herself," Axel said. "The BMW?"

"Oh," Ryan said. "Yeah, Grandma Stevenson was going to have you look at her old car. But she decided to keep it after all. Anyway, it's an old Volvo, not a BMW."

The doors on the elevator began to close.

"My mistake," Axel said, sticking his hand in the doors to catch them. "Have a good one."

Ryan headed down the hallway toward the ER where he worked.

Axel gestured for Delilah to get onto the elevator and he stepped in too.

"That's weird about the car," he said to himself.

"It just appeared?" she asked.

"Yeah, it's the damnedest thing," he said. "I can't remember who might have mentioned they were dropping it off. And Bill swears no one called on it either. I feel like we would have remembered a beamer."

"You should probably call the police," Delilah said.

"The police?" he asked.

"It's not supposed to be there," she said. "It seems fishy."

"They left the keys," he said.

"But no one called?" she asked.

"No," he said, wondering what other reason someone could have for dropping off a car without saying a word. "But this is typical Tarker's Hollow stuff. I'll bet someone dropped it off and thought I would know since they mentioned it to me months ago. I don't want to embarrass anyone by making the cops track down one of my neighbors."

Delilah shrugged, but before she could reply the elevator doors slid open and they headed toward the pediatrician's office.

"Welcome back," the nurse said with a friendly smile. "It's great to see both of you here this time."

Oh dear lord, she though Delilah was Noah's mother.

Axel grimaced inwardly at the awkwardness.

"Nice to meet you," Delilah said smoothly. "I'm Delilah, Noah's new nanny. I'm really glad to be here."

"I'm glad you're here too, dear," the nurse said with a friendly smile. "Come on back."

Axel followed them, wondering at how easy things seem to be with Delilah around.

Mine, said his bear.

Instead of squelching the idea, Axel found himself actually considering it.

Maybe, he replied. *Maybe...*

12

DELILAH

Delilah followed Axel into the shop, cradling baby Noah in her arms.

Noah was contentedly nibbling the head of his favorite rubber giraffe.

Axel was smiling and greeting his apprentice.

Business as usual.

Only Delilah felt a bead of cold sweat running down her back.

You have to do this. It was the whole point...

"Any luck finding the owner of the car?" she asked, hoping her voice sounded natural. She used to be so smooth.

I used to not care about anything but the con.

"Nothing," Bill said. "Isn't that weird? If it was my car I'd have called in by now."

Axel sighed, his troubled expression telling Delilah he was still trying to figure out who the owner was.

"You should really call the police," she reminded him. "They can clear this up quickly. They'll just run the plate."

"She's right," Bill said, nodding approvingly. "We need to know who it belongs to."

"I guess you're right," Axel said at last.

He slipped his phone out of his pocket and dialed.

"He listens to you," Bill said to Delilah, raising his eyebrows.

"He listens to *us*," she said conspiratorially.

That earned her a wink.

The apprentice could be a good ally. But that wasn't why she felt pleased.

She was suddenly anxious to be accepted in this world, for however short a time.

The person Axel was speaking with was shouting so loudly she could hear the voice through his phone from across the shop, though she couldn't make out any individual words.

She wasn't sure what was wrong, but Delilah's stomach cramped with fear.

"Sure, come on out," Axel said.

He hung up and came over to join them.

"He sounded upset," she said lightly.

"Who? Dale?" Axel asked.

Bill chuckled.

"What?" Delilah asked.

"He's just gone a little deaf is all," Axel said.

"And he seems to think the rest of us have too," Bill added with a smile. "So he always shouts."

Delilah smiled back and brushed a kiss on the top of Noah's head.

Axel pulled on a coverall, rolled up his sleeves and began changing the oil of an SUV, discussing shop business with Bill as he worked.

Delilah carried the baby over to the Mustang and

glanced over it.

The car was even more beautiful than she had thought before. Every inch of chrome glistened.

She slipped her phone out of her pocket and tried taking a surreptitious picture.

She was roused by the sound of a car pulling up in the gravel lot.

Axel slid out from under the SUV quickly.

Delilah scrambled to slip her phone back into her pocket before he could see it, cursing herself for getting it out at all when he was around. She'd told him she didn't have one. How would she explain it to him if he spotted it?

His eyes stayed on her for an extra moment.

"Wow, they don't waste any time around here," she said brightly, indicating the older officer climbing out of the police car in the lot.

"There's not much else to do," Axel replied.

She tried to convince herself he hadn't seen her phone. But there was something a little flat in his tone.

"Where's this mystery car, son?" the officer shouted.

"Hey there," Axel called back, walking out to greet him.

Delilah stayed where she was, willing herself to blend into the background.

She couldn't quite bear to sneak back to the cottage, though she probably should do just that. She really wanted to make sure the BMW made its way back to the busboy's uncle.

Axel came in with the portly policeman.

"Who's this pretty little thing?" the cop bellowed.

Delilah felt her face turning pink.

"Oh, this is Noah's new nanny, her name is Delilah," Axel said politely. "Delilah, this is Officer Evans."

"That's Dale to you, honey," the man shouted happily.

"Nice to meet you," she said as loudly and clearly as she could.

Dale beamed back at her.

"Here's the car," Axel said, guiding the officer over to the BMW.

"What was wrong with it?" Dale asked.

"Nothing that I could find," Axel said. "I went ahead and did a courtesy check and an oil change, like I would for anyone. Otherwise, I can't think why someone would drop it off."

"Interesting," Dale said, nodding his head. "It doesn't look familiar, does it?"

"Nope," Axel said.

They gazed at the car together.

Run the plates, run the plates, Delilah thought to herself madly, but kept her mouth shut.

"Let me run the plates real fast," Dale said.

He jotted the number down and trotted out to his vehicle.

"Nice of him to help out," Axel said. "I know I'm going to smack my forehead when he comes back here and tells me whose it is."

But a moment later Dale reappeared with a funny expression.

"Darnedest thing," he said. "Pennsylvania plates, but it's owned by some corporation out in Glacier City. Can't make heads nor tails of it."

"Really?" Axel asked.

Delilah tried to hide her surprise. She'd been expecting the name of a little old man, certainly not an out-of-state corporate owner.

"Maybe it's a rental company?" Axel asked.

"Doesn't sound like it," Dale said doubtfully. "Glacier

City Ship and Transfer Concern, Inc.?"

"Huh," Axel said.

"Why don't you just check your security footage?" Dale suggested.

"Oh shoot, I forgot I even had that," Axel said, shaking his head.

Dale laughed a big belly laugh.

"Well, I don't exactly remember how to check that thing, and I'm a little messy right now," Axel said, indicating his hands and coverall. "But I'll check it out tonight after I get cleaned up and put the baby to bed."

"Let me know who it was," Dale said. "Now I'm curious too."

"I sure will," Axel replied. "Thank you again for coming by so quick. Do you want a soda or anything for the road? The fridge is stocked."

"No can do," Dale said sadly. "Lana's got me on a strict diet."

"She loves you," Axel said. "She wants to keep you around as long as possible."

"I guess so," Dale said, brightening. "See you all later."

Delilah watched him go, her face frozen in a polite expression as her world dropped out from under her.

Security footage?

She was caught.

She glanced around and spotted the camera. A small black dome under the outside floodlights. How had she missed that?

Her mind raced through ways to escape without endangering Noah by leaving him alone in the cottage. She would have to wait until tonight.

Somehow, the idea of leaving him at all felt like something ripping inside her chest.

13

AXEL

After work, Axel took a walk. He peeled off his clothes as soon as he was out of sight of the path that had led him deep into the college woods.

One good thing about having a live-in nanny was that he had been able to duck out right after he finished work.

Now he was finally going to be able to shift and run in the woods as he had burned to do in the months since Noah's birth.

The cool air felt good against his heated skin and the scent of the pine trees called to him.

It would be good to shift, good to escape the questions swirling in his mind.

Why would she lie to me?

He thought back to the hurt expression in her eyes when he'd told her he wanted to go for a jog instead of eating dinner with her.

She lied, he reminded himself.

The bear felt his anger and called to him, a song of comfort.

She cares for the cub.

It was true.

Even though she had lied to him, Axel trusted her implicitly with Noah. Her bond with the baby was clear, he knew he didn't need to worry.

It was his own heart he had to look out for.

Let me carry you, the bear offered hopefully.

Well, the bear was going to get his wish.

Axel tucked his bundle of clothing into a hollow tree and sank to the forest floor.

He shifted fast and landed hard with the satisfying bulk of the bear upon him.

The scents and sounds of the forest flew at him, filling his senses and transporting him from his daily worries.

When the bear took over, there was only the immediate moment: joy, sorrow, hunger or thirst - each was enough to fill his mind completely.

Right now, the bear was alight with the joy of his sudden freedom.

His muscles gathered and he leapt into the woods, enjoying the compression and release of his limbs and the pleasant scratch of the underbrush against his shaggy coat.

He thundered along a familiar route, pausing to snuffle for berries in all the usual spots, though summer was long gone.

The sweet scent of flowing water drew him closer to the creek. When he reached it, he plunged his snout into the stream and drank his fill.

Axel had always loved being outside. He'd been close with Chance Harkness growing up, and the two of them would spend half their summers at Harkness Farms, wandering in the fruit patches and playing hide and seek in the cut-your-own Christmas tree forest.

After he shifted for the first time, being outside became almost a religious experience.

The air he'd always thought was clear was actually a tapestry of all the places he loved - the woods, the creek, the metallic tang of the railroad tracks leading to Philadelphia, the scent of a hundred meals being cooked in town.

He still heard the rush of the breeze and the song of the cicadas. But now he also heard the footsteps of birds and toads, the hush of the highway, and even the notes of Harry Dross's piano floating out the window to him from way over on Elm Avenue.

The world whispered its secrets to Axel. All he had to do was listen.

From across the woods and college fields he felt the pull of his mate bond, stretched thin and taut by the distance between them.

He smacked his lips for the last taste of crystalline water and then turned back toward the path.

He had been gone from the woman and child longer than he could bear. It was time to return.

He loped back into the trees, moving quickly and quietly for one so large.

The tension inside him began to subside as he drew closer to home.

Somewhere in the background of his own consciousness, Axel recognized that the bear was staking claims, whether he was ready for them or not.

They had reached an outcropping of rock from which he could look down and see half the town spread out before him. From this ridge he could even see his own cottage.

A light was on in the shop.

14

DELILAH

Delilah cradled sleepy Noah in one arm as she frantically searched the hard drive of the shop's computer.

Axel had said he was going for a run, but she had no idea how long he would be gone. She knew he was in good shape, so she guessed she had some time.

She had given him a ten-minute head start in case he forgot something and came back in. Then she'd taken the baby and headed for the shop.

Picking the lock had been far too easy. His insurance company was going to give him hell about his security when the Mustang went missing, that was for sure.

But if she'd thought she was going to have an easy time after that, she was wrong.

The shop computer was a mess. She was beginning to wonder if she would ever find the security system software.

The desktop was covered in files, as if Axel had never heard of a folder.

There were about a thousand pictures of Noah at

various ages, and it was impossible not to be distracted by them.

Hundreds of photos of a familiar-looking Noah smiling were layered over pictures of him on Axel's chest in a sling. Below those Noah's tiny pink face was wrinkly and his little body was wrapped in a hospital blanket.

She forced herself to keep looking for the security footage - though all she wanted was to pore over Axel's memories of Noah.

Beneath those were one or two pictures of a blonde woman, who she figured must be Noah's mom.

She studied the pretty face, wondering again how she could have left. As far as Delilah could see, a life with Axel and Noah would have been an uncomplicated heaven for this lucky woman.

None of my business, she told herself and tried to concentrate on looking for the security footage.

She had just uncovered the icon of a camera when she got the feeling that someone was watching her.

She scanned the windows of the shop, but it was dark out there and she'd needed to turn on a light inside to get to the computer.

Noah whimpered in his sleep and she nuzzled his warm head.

"Sleep, sleep, baby," she murmured, turning back to the monitor.

A few quick keystrokes were all she needed...

The back door opened, and heavy footsteps headed her way.

"Hello," Axel called from the darkness.

"Uh, hey," she called back, praying the monitor would go back to sleep before he reached her.

It went blessedly dark just as he stepped into the lobby.

Delilah's mouth dropped open as she took him in.

Axel's t-shirt clung to his body, and he was damp, almost as if he had been swimming. His sweats were slightly askew.

But it was the heated expression in his icy blue eyes that threw her the most.

"I c-couldn't find Noah's giraffe," she managed to stammer. "And I remembered he had it in here earlier."

He stared at her without speaking.

"And here it is," she said brightly, bending to pick it up.

Years of practice at sleight of hand allowed her to slide the rubber toy out of her jacket and make it look like it had been on the floor all along.

"I guess it's time for bed," she prattled in pretend happiness, wandering back to the door to head to the cottage.

After a moment she heard his footsteps behind her and breathed a sigh of relief.

She'd had just enough time to slide a bunch of the pictures back on top of the icon. If he was as much of a slob with that computer as she thought he was, he wouldn't suspect a thing.

"Get some sleep," he said, his voice rough. "You guys have play group tomorrow."

"Okay," she said, trying not to be too disappointed that they weren't going to have a repeat of last night.

He had seen her phone earlier - he must have.

She knew she could make up something - anything - to explain why she had lied about not having a phone before.

But somehow she just couldn't bring herself to lie to him again.

When they reached the cottage, he opened the door for her.

"Do you want me to put him to bed?" he offered.

"No, no, go eat your dinner," she told him. "I left you a plate in the microwave."

"Thanks," he told her and headed to the kitchen.

She carried Noah upstairs and opened the door to his little room.

He fussed a little when she placed him gently in the crib, but she rubbed his little belly just like she's seen Axel do last night and the baby sighed and drifted back into a deep sleep.

She watched over him for a moment, loving everything about him: the tiny chest rising and falling, fists clenched, almost-invisible eyelashes kissing those chubby cheeks.

Then she forced herself to go back to her own room.

She changed into the pajamas they'd picked up on the way home from the doctor's office, and brushed her teeth, then climbed in between the sheets.

She could just see the twinkling stars through the branches of the big maple.

She thought about Axel's eyes - twinkling warmly at her last night, flashing angrily tonight.

And his clothes had been half-drenched and askew.

Oh, Delilah, you idiot.

Of course. He hadn't been going for a jog. He'd probably gone off for a quickie with whoever he was actually dating.

The idea stung, even though she had no claim over him.

Tears prickled her eyelids.

Go to sleep, she told herself firmly.

But she tossed and turned for a long time before sleep took her.

15

DELILAH

Delilah climbed the stairs of the Tarker's Hollow Community Center the next morning with Noah on her hip.

He was crowing with delight and banging her shoulder with his little fists, like he knew exactly where they were headed and couldn't wait to get there.

Delilah enjoyed his enthusiasm, but she was feeling a little less confident herself.

It was one thing to trick the person who already thought you were a nanny into believing you.

It was another to put yourself out there with the other parents and caregivers. She worried that they would know right away that she wasn't one of them.

Delilah was exceptionally good at fitting in when it came to a con. But somehow she couldn't stop pretending she really was Noah's nanny, wanting to make a good impression on the other moms.

Up until now, it had always felt like playing a part. But this part was starting to feel way too real.

"Welcome to Playgroup," a woman's voice chimed with

false cheerfulness just as Delilah reached the top of the steps.

Delilah braced herself. But before she had even replied, help appeared on the scene.

"Hey there," a man said kindly. "You must be Noah's new nanny."

"Thank you," she said to the small blonde woman who had welcomed her, then turned to the man.

He was tall with dark hair. A little boy trotted up behind him to lean on his leg and peek out at her.

"Yes, I'm Delilah," she told the man.

"I'm Bane," he said. "And this is my son, Oliver. Say hi, Ollie."

Oliver's eyes grew large and he darted off to play with a pretend stove.

Delilah laughed and Bane grinned down at her.

"Axel and Noah normally hang out with us," he said. "Or at least so I'm told. Wednesday was my first day."

He led her to a sunny corner of the enormous room, where two other guys had three babies between them.

"Guys, this is Delilah," Bane told them. "Delilah, this is Chase and Dax."

She nodded at them, hoping she would remember the guy with the long dark hair was Chase and that the blond was Dax.

"So how's the new gig?" Chase asked her. "Do you like hanging out with Noah?"

His tone was playful enough that it felt like they'd known each other forever.

Delilah felt her shoulders go down a little as some of the tension left her.

"It's amazing, are you kidding?" she asked. "Axel and Noah are the best."

"Axel?" Dax echoed, sounding surprised.

"Yeah," Delilah said. "He's a great dad and he's been really great showing me the ropes."

"Wow," Dax replied.

"We're only surprised because we figured with you around, he'd be spending all his free time with Sally," Chase explained.

"Sally?" she echoed stupidly.

"Yeah," Dax said. "I'm surprised you've seen him at all. Sally is his obsession."

The others all laughed.

It hit her at once. Of course. Sally must be the woman he was dating.

She must have been who he'd run off to see last night.

Delilah immediately felt guilty for kissing him the other night. No wonder he hadn't wanted anything in return.

If she'd known he was dating someone, she would never have let any of it happen.

"So what do you think of Tarker's Hollow?" Dax asked kindly.

"Oh, it's such a sweet place," Delilah said automatically. "I can't believe how safe it is, and how nice everyone is."

"Can you please write that down for Bane?" Chase asked her. "I think he needs a reminder of why this place is special."

"I have nothing against Tarker's Hollow," Bane said. "I just wasn't planning to come home quite yet."

"Why did you?" Delilah asked.

Bane's brow furrowed slightly. "My sister died recently," he said. "Ollie is her son. If he can't have her in his life, I figure the next best thing is to grow up in a place where everyone knew how special she was."

"Oh, I'm sorry," Delilah said. "I had no idea."

"How would you?" he asked, giving her a gentle smile. "Anyway, Tarker's Hollow is a magical place, especially for children. I wouldn't want to be anywhere else right now."

Delilah smiled back at him and then turned to watch the other three babies rummaging around in the pile of toys at the center of the blanket.

Noah sat on her knee, waving his arms and cackling at them.

"He wants to play too," Dax said.

"Soon enough, buddy," Chase told him.

"*Bah*," Noah replied throatily.

They all laughed.

"Yeah, he's ready to play," Bane said, nodding.

"Listen guys, if you'll watch Jacob for a minute I'll run to my car," Chase said. "I grabbed us all coffees, but I have to bring them up. I hope you drink coffee, Delilah."

"Yeah, thank you," she said, gratified to be treated like one of the gang.

"Come on, bud," Bane said, putting his arms out for Jacob.

Jacob chuckled and let himself be handed off.

She watched Chase head for the stairs.

"Off the record, we're really glad you're here," Dax told her.

"Yeah?" she said.

"The moms and other caregivers usually give us the cold shoulder," he said. "It's nice to have a woman over here to make us seem more legit."

Bane laughed.

"You don't know, Bane," Dax said. "You haven't been here."

"It's probably just because you guys are hot," Delilah said. "They don't want to be accused of flirting with you."

"We're hot?" Bane asked, grinning.

Dax gave him a friendly shove.

Delilah laughed.

"Whatever their reasons, they kind of pretend like we're not here," Dax said. "But maybe with you around, they'll see we're not so bad."

"Coffee time," Chase announced, bounding up the stairs with a flat of paper coffee cups.

Axel's friends were so nice. She had never felt so instantly accepted before.

The sun came out from behind a cloud and the blanket was bathed in rainbow patterned sunlight from the big windows.

Noah squealed with delight.

Suddenly Delilah had a lump in her throat, sentimental for a beautiful slice of life that was completely out of her reach.

16

AXEL

Axel lay on his bed, looking out the window at the waning moon between the trees.

It had been hard to sleep last night, and tonight was turning out to be even worse.

All he could think of was Delilah.

Somehow, he'd made it calmly through the whole day.

He'd even eaten dinner with her. It was that delicious meatloaf again, as if she were trying to make something up to him.

They'd both focused on Noah and the meal had passed pleasantly without incident.

Outwardly, at least, it had.

Inwardly, Axel's bear was throwing himself against the bars of the cage, desperate to make things right with his mate.

Axel resisted the urge to shift, then and now.

The bear had pretty good instincts, generally. But sometimes the human knew best.

Delilah seemed to have come to the same conclusion.

She hardly made eye contact with him all evening and she seemed oddly embarrassed.

It was a relief when she scrambled upstairs to put Noah to bed and to read.

He happened to know there wasn't a single book in her room.

And she had never gotten her "lost suitcase" back either.

That must have been a lie, too.

Her heart is true, the bear told him.

And although he was probably an idiot for agreeing, he knew it was so. In spite of everything that didn't make sense about Delilah, the one thing that was clear was her obvious tenderness with Noah, and her kindness to Axel.

A small sound from downstairs roused his bear.

Axel sat up and listened.

It was a clicking, wrenching sound - as if someone were fumbling with a locked door.

He slipped out of bed and made his way to the hallway.

It was dark but his bear lent him keen senses.

He crept down the stairs.

Muffled whispers came from the vicinity of the back door.

"I don't know about this," one male voice murmured. "Out here in the country people have guns and shit."

"Shut up, Sweet Tea, I'm trying to work," another voice hissed.

"Do you really think Vinny will get us a job with his uncle for this?" the voice that belonged to the one called Sweet Tea whined.

"Fuck his uncle," the other one spat. "I've almost got it."

They were breaking into his house.

The very thought was so alien, he almost didn't know how to process it.

His house.

Where his baby and mate were sleeping.

The bear began to shudder inside Axel, his chest aching with an unvoiced roar, fur threatening to bristle through his skin.

Steady, he told himself.

He made his way into the kitchen stood in the threshold as the door finally opened with a pop.

Two young men stood on the other side.

One was tall and skinny, the other shorter and stockier.

They were both dressed like thugs from a movie, wearing dark, hooded clothing with gold chains.

The necklaces and their dumbfounded expressions told him all he needed to know.

Serious criminals would never wear jewelry that could make them vulnerable in hand to hand combat.

These men were out of their element.

"Who the hell are you?" Axel growled.

"Look, we don't want no trouble," the shorter one said, sounding like a bad guy right out of central casting.

"If that's true then you shouldn't have started this conversation by breaking and entering," Axel replied.

"Good point, man, good point, good point," the punk replied. "I should have said we don't want no trouble with *you.*"

"Who *do* you want trouble with?" Axel asked, running out of patience.

"We only came for the girl."

His blood thundered in his ears and it took everything he had not to let the bear take over.

"Get out of here now," he growled.

"Just give us the girl and we'll go," the short guy said.

"No way, man, he looks like he's about to hulk out or something," the taller one said.

"Shut up, Sweet Tea," shorty spat, then turned back to Axel. "Give us the girl and we'll be on our way."

But Axel wasn't there anymore.

His clothes were exploding from his expanding form, his face lengthening, fur bursting from his body as he shifted involuntarily for the first time since his adolescence.

"*Fuck*," Sweet Tea yelped, stepping backward so quickly he almost fell over in his haste to escape.

"What the hell?" the other man breathed.

Nooooo, Axel moaned from behind the bars.

The bear turned on the shorter human, threw his head back and roared.

The wannabe thug screamed.

An acrid scent filled the air.

Axel shook his massive head to clear the smell from his sensitive nose.

The man had peed on the floor in terror.

Somewhat mollified by this show of submission, the bear allowed Axel to restrain him.

The man slipped in the puddle of his own pee and crawled for the back door.

Upstairs, Noah began to cry.

The sound was echoed tinnily right behind Axel.

He whipped around.

Delilah stood in the living room, the baby monitor clutched to her chest.

He reached out instantly with his senses.

The sound of an engine told him the thugs had made it to their car and were trying to escape.

Although he would have liked to have loped outside to

chase them down, the bear stepped back, allowing Axel to shift back into human form.

Comfort our mate.

Axel closed his eyes for the shift and felt the sounds of the world fade as the coolness of the room registered on his bare skin.

"Delilah," he said softly, opening his eyes.

She still stood before him clutching the monitor, her eyes wide with fear.

"I know that was scary," he said carefully.

"Y-you turned into a bear," she said.

"I'm a shifter," he said. "It means I can turn into a bear."

She didn't reply.

"I'm still me," he assured her. "Even in bear form I would never hurt you."

She nodded, still staring at him, lips slightly parted.

"I'm sure you have questions," he said.

She didn't speak, but Axel waited, willing her curiosity to win out over her fear.

She should have found out another way. I should have had the chance to tell her, when she knew me better...

"It makes sense now," she said at last.

"I seemed like a bear to you?" he asked, fascinated.

"No, it makes sense why you don't bother locking doors," she said.

Her words hung in the air for a moment.

Then Axel began to laugh.

When her soft laughter joined his, Axel felt his heart click together, as if it had been in pieces until that moment.

Mine.

He stepped toward her instinctively, ready to hold her, to confess his love.

He didn't care what her secrets were, he would hear them when she was ready to tell him.

All he knew was that he was hers now. He had been a fool to worry about the rest.

But she stepped back, arms lifted as if he were holding a weapon.

"I-I'm sorry," he stammered, taking a step back.

"I'd better check on Noah," she muttered, dashing up the stairs.

Axel stood naked in his living room for a long time, listening to the soft sounds of his mate comforting his child in the room above.

He wondered if she had already realized that Noah carried the same shifter heritage in his blood.

She probably hadn't. Surely she was still in shock.

He wondered if she would leave right away when she realized, or if she'd give him time to find another nanny.

The house felt empty already.

And Axel's chest felt hollow.

Mate, the bear insisted.

No, he told it sadly. *Not this one.*

17

DELILAH

Delilah was both sad and relieved to find Axel was gone by the time she got herself and baby Noah up and dressed.

Seeing him last night had made everything so much harder. Her resolve had nearly slipped.

He's a bear. He's a freaking bear...

It was like something out of one of her favorite childhood books: a kind and gentle man, who shifted into a wild creature when the moon was full, or his friends were in danger.

Delilah had never imagined that such a thing could be real.

But then she had seen it with her own eyes.

She felt like she ought to be freaked out by the whole situation, but for some reason, it all seemed perfectly natural.

In fact, if she was being honest, it was pretty damn cool.

And even though it should have been frightening, she had never felt safer.

She packed Noah into his stroller, and they walked into the village. Delilah was in a complete daze, picturing a world in which she came home to a baby like Noah and a man who could protect them from *anything*.

"He's got a girlfriend," she mumbled to herself sternly. "How would Sally feel about your crush?"

"*Bah*," Noah said, kicking his feet in his stroller as if in agreement.

"I know, buddy," she said. "I'm trying to do the right thing."

She figured Axel must be feeling pretty crummy today. Those two guys he'd saved her from were a surprise to her, but they must have been a complete shock to him.

She knew the Barracuda was serious about the car, but sending thugs was not her MO. And if it were, she wouldn't send half-rate ones like that.

It didn't make any sense.

Delilah had called her twice already this morning, but it went straight to voicemail.

Delilah shivered at the idea that anyone would be coming after her when Noah was in the house.

And then Axel had been forced to show his other self last night...

She sighed and did the backwards trick to get herself and Noah in the door of the coffee shop and bought two cappuccinos before she could talk herself out of it.

On the way home she called the Barracuda again, but nobody picked up.

When she reached the shop, she took a deep breath.

You're going to try to make things right with him, she told herself. *But you're not going to throw yourself at him.*

"Hey, there," Bill called to her.

"Hi," she said. "I got you guys some coffee."

"Oh, Axel's not here," Bill said. "He had to take a run for parts."

She hated the forlorn feeling that instantly descended on her.

He's not your boyfriend. You don't get to miss him.

She shrugged and headed over to Bill with one of the coffees.

"Thanks, Delilah," he said, taking it.

Sunlight was slanting through the windows, sending rainbow sparkles off the Mustang's candy apple paint job.

She walked over to it, unable to resist.

"Pretty, isn't it?" Bill asked.

"Yeah," she said, walking all the way around until she spotted the vanity plate.

SALLY 67

"SALLY," she said out loud.

We figured with you around he'd be spending all his free time with Sally... Sally is his obsession...

"It's the car," she realized out loud.

But the car belonged to some rich client. Why would Axel be obsessed with it?

"What?" Bill asked.

"Nothing," she said. "Um, who does Sally belong to?"

"Sally?" Bill asked. "Oh, she's Axel's pride and joy. He puts all his free time into her. At least, he *used to.*" He gave her a wink.

"Didn't you say the guy who owned her had ten others just like it in his garage?" she asked.

"Ha," Bill barked. "Not the car, can you imagine having

ten of *that?* No, I was talking about the hog-ring pliers Axel borrowed for the upholstery."

He indicated a red-handled tool on the bench near the car.

"Oh," Delilah said, unable to think of another word.

"Ten of them," Bill said to himself, chuckling as he bent over the car he was working on again.

Axel didn't have a girlfriend.

He had a car.

Delilah's heart soared at the thought, but crashed back down at the immediate realization that followed.

A car the Barracuda was about to steal.

No, no, no...

She hurried back to the house, determined to reach her partners and come up with a compromise.

It was lucky that Noah was there to keep her grounded.

She fed him and then chatted with him while she cleaned the kitchen. She was going to make Axel a meal tonight herself, even if it wasn't as good as the stuff from his favorite restaurant. She would take Noah to the library this afternoon and find a cookbook. They would stop by the Co-op for fresh ingredients and if she bumped into that nice Eva Cortez again, she would tell her the truth about her cooking abilities and ask for advice.

There was a bang on the back door.

Suddenly all of Delilah's plans were out the window.

She lifted Noah from his jumperoo and held him close, backing toward the front door and hoping they could make it to the shop before whoever this was realized she was gone.

But the back door slammed open with a crash before she could make it out of the room.

"Delilah," the Barracuda's voice sounded rustier and crasser than ever in the coziness of Axel's homey kitchen.

"Y-you're here," Delilah stammered. "I've been trying to reach you all day."

The Barracuda stepped in, glaring at her with frosty blue eyes, a pinched expression highlighting the wrinkles in her forehead.

"Let me guess, you lost the second car, but there's a bridge you want us to buy," Hank sneered. His huge form nearly filled the doorway.

Delilah was furious, but she could not forget for an instant that Noah was in her arms.

"I'd like to speak with her alone," she said calmly.

"I don't think so," Hank laughed bitterly. "You made us track you all the way to this godforsaken burg. Anything you want to say to her you can say to me too."

"Fine. You can't have the car," she said, looking directly into those piercing blue eyes. "I'm sorry you came all the way here, but I'm out. I'm completely out of the game. And I'm not coming back."

"Bull shit," the older woman said, enunciating each syllable.

"I haven't asked much of you over the years," Delilah said. "You moved me around, you took me out of school, you made me pull cons with you when I was too young to even know what a con was. It ends today. I'm still your daughter, but I'm not your partner anymore."

The Barracuda's mouth dropped open slightly.

Delilah studied her mother's face for a whisper of compassion.

"So you're trying to pull the family card now?" Hank spat.

"Shut up, Hank," Delilah said. "This is between her and me."

"Don't you tell him to shut up," the woman shrieked,

clearly choosing her side. "I taught you everything you know, Delilah. And if you think you're *ever* going to be anything more than a lousy con, then you're a bigger idiot than I thought."

"Please," Delilah said quietly. "Just leave."

"I wish you could see how ridiculous you look," the Barracuda said. "You're playing house, carrying around that baby. Do you know what he's going to do when he finds out what you are?"

"He's not going to find out because you're going to leave *right now*," Delilah said.

"Like hell she is," Hank retorted. "I've been subsidizing your stupid conscience with shitty gigs since the day I partnered up with your mother. You're leaving with us, we're taking the car, and from here on in we're doing things *my* way. No more of your stupid rules. From now on, it's go big or go home."

"She is home," a deep male voice said from the front door.

"Axel," Delilah gasped.

"Who the hell do you think you are?" Axel demanded, stalking into the room.

"I'm her mother," the Barracuda sniffed. "And she's only here to con you. She invited us here to steal that Mustang in your shop."

"I can't believe you let her take care of your baby," Hank laughed. "You poor dumb bastard."

Delilah choked back a huge sob and pressed Noah into his father's arms.

She ran out the front door, trying not to listen to the angry conversation taking place in the kitchen.

She had to get out, to get away. She couldn't face Axel's fury now that he knew the truth.

She wanted to remember him smiling at her, his twinkly blue eyes happy and trusting.

18

DELILAH

Delilah paced the platform at the Tarker's Hollow train station.

The wind had picked up a little, scattering flame-colored leaves along the paving stones.

The clock tower told her she had three minutes until the train arrived that would carry her to Philadelphia.

Three more minutes to soak in this sweet town and the life she had lived here.

She looked out over the little village.

The hardware store guy was setting out a display of rakes and leaf bags in front of his store. A woman walking past waved at him and he stopped to chat with her.

A woman jogged toward the station, dressed like she was ready to shop until she dropped in the city.

An elderly gentleman tipped his cap to a group of women with strollers who were headed into the Co-op.

It looked like a movie set, but it felt more real than all the other experiences of her life.

She would carry it with her always.

The wind changed and she caught the scent of the coffee brewing at *Edible Complex* next to the station.

Instantly she pictured Noah in his stroller, chattering happily up at her as they waited in line.

He's going to grow up. He's going to grow up and I'm going to miss it.

Her eyes burned with unshed tears, but she set her jaw, determined not to cry. That future had never been hers to begin with. So why did it feel like it was being stolen from her?

Two minutes.

She should have been on this train five days ago. She never would have tasted this life she couldn't have. It would have been better for her. Better for everyone.

No. That was a lie. It wouldn't have been better.

Even though her heart was breaking, Delilah was glad she had come to Tarker's Hollow, glad she had known Noah and Axel.

They had taught her that there was another way to live.

It was going to be a long road, but she was determined to change her life.

If she could forge her way forward without relying on her more unsavory skills, maybe one day she would have a family of her own, one she deserved.

But she couldn't bring herself to picture that.

All she saw when she closed her eyes was Axel and Noah.

One minute.

She could hear the rumble of the train's approach.

And someone calling her name.

"Delilah," Axel's voice cried hoarsely.

She stepped away from the tracks and scanned the town.

He was on the sidewalk beside the café, running for her like his life depended on it.

When he caught sight of her his face went soft with relief.

"What are you doing?" he demanded.

"I'm leaving," she told him, the words like broken glass in her mouth.

"I didn't mean to freak you out the other night," he said. "I never should have let you see me like that without preparing you first. But I guess now you know what I really am."

"How could you think this has anything to do with what you are?" she demanded. "That was the most amazing thing I've ever seen."

"Then why?" he asked.

"It's because now you know what I really am," she said. "I tricked you. It's what I do. You can turn into a bear, but I'm the one who's a monster. I'm the one who dropped that car off."

The train arrived, sending the leaves on the platform dancing.

"I already knew that," he said, shaking his head.

"How?" she asked.

"I watched the security footage before you swiped it," he told her.

She blinked at him in wonder.

"All aboard for Philadelphia, 30th Street Station," a voice said over the speakers.

"I have to go," she said.

"You aren't going anywhere," he told her.

"If you knew, why did you still keep me around? How could you trust me with Noah?" she asked, her curiosity getting the better of her.

"You're a good person," he told her. "That much was clear to me."

"How can you know that I'm a good person," she asked.

"I just felt it," he said simply. "I have better instincts than most."

He gave her a significant look.

The bear.

Holy crap, the *bear* knew she wasn't dangerous?

Somehow, that made perfect sense.

"Why didn't you ask me why I left the car?" she asked, grasping at straws.

"I figured you'd tell me when you were ready," he said, looking down at his boots. "It's not like you were the only one with a secret. The last person I confronted ran off. I couldn't lose you too. It would kill me. But more importantly, it would make Noah really sad."

The tears Delilah had held back earlier flew out of her eyes before she could stop them.

"I'm so sorry," she sobbed.

His arms were around her instantly. "Please don't go," he murmured into her hair. "Don't ever go."

"I won't, I won't," she repeated, clinging to him.

The train pulled out of the station and the leaves swirled in its wake once again as Delilah relaxed at last in Axel's arms.

19

AXEL

Axel drove home with his hand wrapped around Delilah's.

He didn't dare let go of her for a moment. It was still too delicate, too tenuous, this bond between them.

Delilah leaned against her seat, facing him, still teary-eyed.

He hoped he would never see her cry again, except maybe with happiness. It would be his mission to make her happy, to keep his family safe.

He drove all the way down to the cottage and parked in front.

"I'm just going to run and get Noah," he told her. "Would you mind starting his bottle? I'll bet he's hungry."

He felt terrible using his son to trick her, but he couldn't let her into the shop again just yet. Not until he was sure she knew how much he cared about her.

"I'll come with you," she said. "It'll only take a minute to make his bottle."

"Don't bother," he said. "I've gotta give Bill instructions on Dulcie Blanco's car, it's a little tricky."

"No worries," she said, heading into the shop. "I'll bring Noah back for his bottle if you guys have a lot to do."

Shit, he said to himself, watching her walk through the back door of the shop.

He jogged to catch up with her.

She was taking Noah from Bill when he joined her.

"Hey buddy," she said tenderly to Noah, who promptly banged the top of her head with his little hand in approval.

"*Bah*," he crowed, and grabbed a hank of her hair.

Axel wasn't the only one who never wanted to let her out of his sight.

He saw the exact moment when she turned and noticed the car was missing. It didn't take her long to connect the dots.

"Sally," she said, her face stricken. "Oh, Axel, no."

"It doesn't matter," he told her honestly.

"Of course it matters," she said plaintively. "Why would you let them take it?"

"Walk with me," he told her.

She went to him reluctantly and he led her back out to the gravel path.

"You worked so hard on that car," she said. "It was beautiful."

"It doesn't matter, at all," he told her. "It was a small price to pay to keep you safe."

"To keep me safe?" she asked.

"They agreed never to contact you again," he told her. "Which is not to say that you can't contact them if you wanted to. She's your family."

"Not really," Delilah said, unconsciously brushing the top of Noah's head with her lips. "Not anymore."

His heart sang at the sweet gesture.

"Well, in any case, they won't be asking you to do jobs with them anymore," Axel told her. "We can relax."

"I didn't want you to give up Sally for me," she said.

He stopped and placed a hand on her shoulder.

"Delilah, that car was just an escape," he told her. "Things in my life were topsy-turvy. The car felt like something I could put back together even when everything else was falling apart."

Her dark eyes were locked on his, an expression of understanding dawning on her beautiful face.

"Now, when I think about my life, Delilah, I don't feel so much like escaping anymore," he told her.

She went up on her toes and wrapped an arm around his neck, cradling Noah between them.

He inhaled the scent of her, trying to memorize the feeling of the three of them all cuddled together.

"*Ha*," Noah crowed, and nuzzled his little nose into Axel's chest.

"Let's go home," Delilah said softly.

Home.

"Yes," he told her. "But I have a feeling that when we do, I'm not going to want to leave again. I was going to run out and pick up some parts for the car we just got in. I'll do that and get Bill set up for his shift. Then you and I can have the whole rest of the day to ourselves. Sound good?"

"That sounds amazing," she said, tilting her head up to smile at him.

He leaned down and pressed his lips to hers gently, loving the softness of her sweet mouth and the tiny sound of satisfaction she made.

The bear groaned with a need to claim her.

Tonight, he promised his other self.

Tonight she will be ours.

20

DELILAH

Delilah carried Noah into the house in a happy haze.

She was finally out of the con game - something she hadn't even known she wanted, but now it seemed like everything to her.

Axel wanted her to stay.

She had been fantasizing about this fairy tale since the hour she'd arrived in the cottage behind the shop. But now that it seemed to be coming true, she couldn't believe it.

This is my life now, she told herself as she carried Noah into the kitchen and started his bottle.

He leaned his warm head against her chest, and she walked him back and forth in front of the big window that overlooked the side of the property.

A cardinal landed in the bushes and sang long and loud, as if he were celebrating with her.

When Noah's meal was ready, she fed him with joy in her heart. He fell asleep in her arms as soon as the bottle was empty.

She took him up to his room and her gaze rested for a

moment on the rocking chair. She wanted nothing more than to hold him and rock him until he woke up. But she knew she'd better take advantage of his nap to use the bathroom and do a little tidying up.

She was just finishing up in the bathroom when she heard him cry.

"Hang on, buddy, I'll be right there," she called to him. "You're okay."

She washed her hands in record time and was wiping them off on her jeans as she went back into his room.

At first it took a moment to put together what was happening.

A man was holding Noah.

But it wasn't Axel.

Sunlight streamed in the window behind the man, illuminating a head of white-blond hair down to his shoulders. He wore an expensive-looking suit that accentuated his long, lean form.

"You must be Delilah," he said in a measured tone that sent chills down her spine. "My name is Roman Panchenko. I believe you have something that belongs to me."

Roman Panchenko.

Roman Panchenko, the infamous head of the Glacier City mob. There wasn't a con artist alive that would dream of getting on the wrong side of the man that now stood before her.

Delilah's hands began to shake.

"Give him to me," she said firmly, her icy words belying her terror.

"He was crying," Panchenko said innocently.

"*Mah,*" Noah whimpered.

"Give him to me," Delilah said, holding out her arms.

To her immense relief, Panchenko shrugged elegantly and handed Noah to her.

"I'm not a monster," he said, the hint of a terrible smile pulling up one corner of his mouth. "I would never hurt a baby."

The words were less of a reassurance, and more of an implication of all the other things he would be willing to do.

Delilah did not want to find out what they were.

"What do you want?" she asked, holding Noah close.

"Where is my car?" Panchenko asked in reply.

"Your car?" she echoed.

"Come, now," he said impatiently. "Let's not play this game. I know you have the BMW. Let's cut to the chase."

Delilah's jaw dropped. "*You're* Vinny's uncle?"

"Please don't mention that insufferable boy," he said, rolling his eyes. "He fell for the oldest con in the book trying to impress me."

"The fiddle game," Delilah said, realizing.

"The fiddle game," Panchenko agreed. "And I guess you played it convincingly. The boy really thought I'd be happy to see that ridiculous flute. Did you even pay a hundred dollars for it?"

"Twenty-five," Delilah said. "But it was another twenty to have it engraved."

"Give me the car and we'll end our conversation here," he said.

He didn't say what would happen if she didn't. He didn't need to.

"Yes," she told him, her heart crashing in her chest. "Absolutely. Come on."

She led him up the gravel drive to the shop, her arms locked around Noah, who was uncharacteristically subdued, most likely sensing her fear.

"Bill," she called out.

"Hey, Delilah," Bill replied. "Oh- hey. Who's this?"

He stared openly at Panchenko and his expensive suit. Delilah guessed there were very few middle-aged men in Tarker's Hollow who looked like a bad guy from *Die Hard*.

"Can you please take Noah and wait outside with him for a minute?" Delilah asked as calmly as she could.

Bill's forehead wrinkled and she prayed that he would agree without making trouble. She couldn't have anything bad happen to Noah or Bill because of her mistakes.

To her relief, Bill came to her right away and took Noah.

"I'll be right outside," he told her, giving her a significant look. "Do you want me to call Axel?"

"*No*," she practically shouted. "I'm fine."

He left quietly.

She turned to Panchenko. "The car is right here, let me grab the keys."

He waited patiently enough while she grabbed the keys off the board behind the desk.

She tossed them to him.

Panchenko deftly snatched them out of the air like a magician.

He pressed the button to unlock the car, but instead of getting in, he opened the trunk.

She watched, fascinated, as he lifted the carpet to reveal a hidden compartment.

Out of the compartment he pulled a small package, wrapped in nondescript brown paper, which he immediately deposited into his coat pocket.

Then he began to pull something else out of his pocket.

Delilah could see metal wink in the sunlight, and she closed her eyes, ready to die, glad that Noah wouldn't see it.

But there was only silence.

She opened her eyes to see that Panchenko was holding out the flute.

He smiled at her ironically and placed it on the roof of the car.

"Pleasure doing business with you," he said, and tossed her back the car keys.

"D-don't you want the car?" she asked, catching the keys automatically.

"I don't care about the car," he told her. "Sell it for parts. I got what I came for." He patted his coat pocket.

"Oh," she said, unable to comprehend what had just happened.

"You seem like a nice kid," Panchenko said, turning back. "Take my advice. No more fiddle game. You have a baby and a legitimate business here."

"No more fiddle game," she echoed stupidly.

"Learn to play the flute," he suggested, "It's a nice instrument."

And with that, he walked out the front door, sending the little bell jingling as if he were a normal customer.

21

AXEL

T he bad feeling grew in Axel's chest from the moment he headed back toward Tarker's Hollow from the Springton Autobody Parts shop.

Something was wrong with Delilah.

Something was very, very wrong.

The bear was storming in his mind, begging him to pull over and let him out.

Driving is faster, he told the desperate creature, speeding up and praying he wouldn't be pulled over.

By the time he pulled into the gravel lot of his own shop his heart was pounding and a cold sweat had formed along his brow.

He leapt out of the station wagon and stormed into the shop.

Bill stood in the lobby holding Noah, a troubled expression on his face.

"Where's Delilah?" Axel demanded.

"She took off in the BMW," Bill said softly.

"Why?" Axel demanded.

"I-I don't know," Bill said. "This man showed up here, in

a suit. And then he left, and she tore out of here a minute later."

Axel sank to the floor, head in his hands.

Find her, go after her, the bear demanded.

But Axel was frozen with despair.

She was gone again. He could chase her again, but if she really wanted to leave, he would never tame her spirit. It would be better to let her go cleanly, for Noah's sake.

She had convinced him that her running away was about her past, but it was clearly about him.

Tears prickled his eyelids and the bear roared in his chest.

There was a screech of tires as a car sailed into the lot and swerved up in front of the shop.

He lifted his face to see a blur of red and a small woman with dark hair burst out of the car, sprinting toward him.

Mine.

He leapt up, arms out for her.

Delilah wrapped herself around him.

"Where did you go?" he asked.

"I had to get Sally back," she told him, pointing proudly out to the lot.

And there was the car.

She was so pleased with herself that he couldn't bear to tell her he would rather she had set it on fire than scare him like that.

"I traded the BMW for her," she told him. "Hank didn't like it, but the Barracuda agreed."

"You call your mother *the Barracuda*?" he asked her.

"Oh, I have so many stories," she told him with a wicked grin.

"And what do you mean you traded the BMW?" he asked. "Was it really yours?"

"You know, I could explain everything," she said. "But it would take a lot of time and, personally, I'd rather start on our new life than gossip about my old one."

"I'll give you something to gossip about," he growled and pulled her in for a kiss.

When he pulled away, he was so overcome with lust he was practically seeing stars.

"Are you in any danger over that BMW?" he managed to ask her. "Bill said there was a man here."

She shook her head. "It's all taken care of. We're out of the woods."

"Bill," he called, still gazing into Delilah's dark eyes. "Any chance you can babysit today? We don't have a big backlog at the shop."

"Oh, sure," Bill said, sounding genuinely thrilled. "I'll take him to the park."

"We're going back to the house," Axel told him.

Bill's eyebrows went straight up, and he looked like he wanted to laugh. But he only nodded and placed Noah in his stroller.

Axel turned to Delilah and swept her up in his arms.

She let out a surprised giggle that made him feel like a superhero.

He couldn't wait to hear the noises she would make when he claimed her at last.

22

AXEL

Axel placed Delilah down gently at the foot of his bed.

They were both already breathless at the thought of what was about to happen.

Delilah was excruciatingly lovely, her eyes soft with need.

"Delilah," he whispered, trying to remember the words he needed to say.

She smiled up at him patiently.

"Delilah, I'm a shifter," he told her.

"I know," she said, her eyes twinkling. "I *saw*. You were incredible."

God, she was beautiful.

"There's something you need to know," he told her. "About being with a shifter."

"Are you going to turn into a bear, during...?" she asked.

He might have laughed at her troubled expression, except that he realized she really thought this might be a possibility. And she was still standing here.

"You're very brave," he told her. "But, no, that's not going to happen."

"Oh, good," she said, relieved. "I mean not that you aren't an attractive bear, it's just…"

"Please don't explain," he told her, smiling. "You don't want to hurt his feelings."

"Can he hear me?" she asked, fascinated.

"Sure," he said. "The bear is always with me, but on the inside, except when I let him out."

"Which is during the full moon?" she asked.

"Sometimes," he said. "I can do it anytime though, any time I need to."

"To protect Noah," she said instantly.

The bear's approving growl echoed in his head.

"Yes," he said. "Or to protect you."

"I'm glad," she said. "I feel safe knowing he's always there."

Claim her now, the bear demanded.

"The thing about the bear is complicated though," Axel said. "Or maybe it's very simple."

"What do you mean?" she asked.

"When he chooses a mate, it's for life," he told her.

"Oh," Delilah said.

"I already know I'm dead serious about you, Delilah," Axel said carefully. "I want to share my life with you forever. But if you don't feel the same, then we should probably just take it slowly and get to know—"

But she cut him off with a gentle kiss that sent white-hot sparks down his spine.

"Are you sure?" he murmured against her mouth.

"Very, very sure," she said, pressing her small, soft form against him.

There was something else he had wanted to say, but it was forgotten.

He meant to take it slowly anyway. He wanted to seduce her carefully, deliberately.

Instead, he found himself tearing off his own clothing and nearly ripping hers in his eagerness to feel her against him.

She laughed and the sweet tinkling sound further incited his lust. He was wild for her, desperate to be inside her, to make his mark on his mate.

When she was naked at last, he nudged her toward the bed.

She crawled in and lay on her back, arms out for him.

The bear groaned with need, responding as much to her submissive posture as to her deliriously inviting scent.

He crawled into the bed and spread her thighs impatiently.

She let her legs fall apart and he buried his face in her fragrant sex, feeding on her sweet juices until she cried out and lifted her hips to meet his mouth.

He pulled back and licked his lips, hands on her trembling thighs.

Delilah was gasping for breath, her lips swollen from his kisses, hair splayed on the pillow, tangled and beautiful.

"Please," she whispered, holding her arms out to him again.

23

DELILAH

Delilah waited in an agony of need as Axel crawled up to her and covered her body with his.

She had never felt this way before, frantic with lust, wholly lost to her desire. But it was more than that. More than just a physical need.

I trust him, she realized. *I trust him implicitly.*

"Are you ready?" he growled, eyes hooded with lust.

"Yes," she said.

Then he was between her thighs, the iron-hard heat of him pressing against her, stretching her slowly, sweetly, until she saw stars.

"Delilah," he groaned into the tender place where her neck met her collarbone.

"Please," she murmured, lifting her hips, knowing she could take him, craving the sensation of him moving inside her.

He growled in surrender and the sensation of the thirst was indescribable - a pain-tinged pleasure that made her toes curl.

She moaned and sank her nails into his shoulders,

clinging to him for fear that she might actually disintegrate from the pleasure.

Axel thrust into her again, each time sending her further and further toward the edge of an abyss of pleasure.

She lifted herself to meet him, lost in a storm of frenzied need.

"Oh, God, Delilah," he groaned.

When she felt his mouth against her neck, she closed her eyes and tried to be still.

There was a moment of pain as his teeth closed on her neck, then nothing but the most exquisite pleasure as he slid a hand between them to circle her most sensitive place.

Delilah lost track of her own sounds as her whole body exploded with an ecstasy so intense she thought she would faint, just as she felt Axel explode inside her, crying out her name.

For a long time, she floated in the throes of unspeakable pleasure, each throb like waves pounding the shoreline.

When the tide finally slowed, she closed her eyes and listened to the rhythm of Axel's rough breath, and the sound of his heartbeat which seemed to reverberate in her very blood.

"*Mine*," he murmured to her.

She swore it was the voice of the bear she heard. But it didn't matter, they were one and the same, two sides of her incredible mate.

"Yours," she agreed as sleep overtook her.

24

AXEL

On Monday morning, Axel sat beside Delilah on the blanket at playgroup with Noah cuddled in his arms.

He and Delilah had opened up early and set everything up together. They had even brought coffee for the whole "single dads" gang.

It was amazing how having Delilah around made everything more fun. Noah had squealed and laughed at her as she played with all the toys they laid out.

But as soon as they sat down to wait for everyone, Delilah seemed to wilt a little.

He glanced over at her now.

She was holding her coffee cup between her palms and biting her plump lower lip.

"Don't be nervous," he told her gently. "The guys already love you. They'll be happy for us."

"Isn't it kind of a cliché?" she asked. "Sleeping with the babysitter?"

"*Imposter* babysitter," he teased. "Although I told the

service we won't be needing the real one after all. And I'm not just *sleeping with you*."

She smiled and he felt his heart leap in his chest. Would he ever get used to this happiness?

Noah yelped joyfully and smacked the top of Axel's head.

Bane was headed up the stairs with Oliver.

"Hey, guys," Bane said. "What's new?"

"Not too much," Axel replied, unable to hide his wide grin.

Bane grinned back.

He knew.

"Well, I'm glad you're both here," Bane said. "How's it going, Delilah?"

"It's going well," she replied smiling at Axel. "It's going really, really well."

Bane laughed and clapped Axel on the back.

"Yeah, yeah, I know I'm grinning like an idiot," Axel laughed. "But I'm happy. I don't care who knows it."

He unwrapped one of Delilah's hands from her coffee cup and squeezed it.

"That's fantastic, man," Bane said genuinely. "I'm really happy for you guys."

"Thank you," Delilah told him. "You look happy today yourself."

"I've decided to do some free-lancing writing gigs," Bane said. "I'll still have a ton of time with Ollie, and it means I won't have to go looking for work."

"Hey, that's great," Axel said, raising his coffee cup in a toasting gesture. "Looks like we all have something to celebrate."

The morning went along as it always did, parents and caregivers arriving, the light streaming in the windows, burnishing the wooden floors and illuminating the happy faces.

Axel's heart threatened to burst as he watched Delilah relax and laugh with his friends. They happily passed baby Noah back and forth between them.

Axel had been struggling to understand the transformation he had seen in his son over the last few days as he enjoyed the undivided attention of twice as many adults as he was accustomed to.

But it came to him now.

Noah was content.

Delilah's inexperience had given Axel greater confidence in his own abilities. And having an extra set of arms around made the whole experience of taking care of a baby more relaxing and enjoyable.

Noah was a perceptive little fellow.

He was happy because his daddy was happy.

Which meant what Axel was about to do much, much easier.

He fingered the edges of the box that was in his pocket, and prayed that Rachel Delgado at the jewelry store hadn't steered him wrong when it came to a choice Delilah would like.

"Hey guys, can you excuse us a minute?" he said.

Everyone looked up.

Delilah looked a little alarmed.

"It's nothing," he said quickly. "Well, it's something. But it's good. I think. Come on."

He cursed himself inwardly - he was as awkward as a teenager around this woman.

She stood with baby Noah in the crook of her arm, and they headed down the stairs together.

The air was fresh and crisp. Dry leaves skidded across

the parking lot, making a whispering sound, as if in antic-ipation.

The breeze blew Delilah's curls and she laughed, which made Noah chuckle and whack her cheek with uncharacter-istic gentleness before leaning his little forehead against her neck.

"I love you so much," Axel heard himself say.

She looked up, surprised, and then looked down at Noah, as if realizing Axel must be talking to the baby.

"Of course I love him," Axel said. "But I was talking to you. I love you, Delilah."

"I love you too," she told him, her lower lip trembling.

He let the words soak in, felt them in his heart, his mind, his very soul.

She smiled at him, exploding the butterflies in his chest and he could bear no more.

He knelt before her, pulling the box from his pocket.

She gasped, her mouth forming a tiny O.

"Delilah, you came into our lives just a few days ago," he said. "But Noah and I... well... we just can't live without you. Will you have us as your family?"

She gazed down at him, her eyes brimming with tears.

"Please, Delilah," he said. "Please marry me."

"Yes," she whispered. "Yes, yes, yes. Except..."

"Except what?" he asked, terrible scenarios popping into his head. Was she unsure about him? Was she already married?

"I, um, I can't cook," she muttered.

"What?" he asked.

"I just, I can't cook," she said. "I can learn. Or at least, I can try, but I don't want to marry you without you knowing the truth."

Axel roared with relieved laughter.

"Is that... funny?" she asked nervously.

"I knew you couldn't cook," he told her. "I recognized the meatloaf right away. But you found out what I liked, and you got it for me. You probably spent all the money I gave you for clothing on meatloaf, didn't you?"

"Most of it," she admitted.

"That was very nice of you," he told her. "And I can't cook either. Maybe we can take a class together?"

Together.

He was starting to really like the sound of that word.

She nodded, smiling back at him again at last.

"Is there anything else I need to know?" he asked her.

"I don't really have any marketable skills," she said miserably. "Unless you wanted to pull a con. And I won't do that anymore. But I don't want to be a burden."

His heart ached. But her words made sense coming from the perspective of a woman whose own mother had pushed her into grifting from the time she was a child.

"I have a successful business, Delilah," he told her gently. "I can't give you luxury, but I can support us. Maybe one day you'll want to take some classes, learn a skill that interests you. I can help you with that too. But only if you want. Noah and I just want you around. You are enough. Just you. Exactly as you are. Do you understand?"

His heart broke as he watched her sob. He stood and put his arms around her, the ring still in his hand.

She rested her head against his chest, and he could feel her tears wet his t-shirt.

Noah nuzzled her neck and grabbed Axel's shirt in a chubby fist.

"Thank you," she whispered at last.

"It's my pleasure," he told her. "But if I can't put this ring on your finger right now, I'm afraid I'm going to combust."

She laughed and pulled back enough for him to slide the ring onto her finger.

The little diamond winked in the morning sun and Delilah gazed at it rapturously.

"You like it?" he asked.

"I love it," she said. "But mostly I love you. Both of you."

"We are all so lucky," he told her.

He bent to kiss her, and she pressed her lips to his so sweetly it made him feel half-dizzy.

"Come on," he whispered to her. "Let's go tell our friends."

She grinned up at him and nodded.

He wrapped an arm around her shoulder and the three of them headed back into the community center to share their joy with their friends, and to begin the rest of their lives.

Together.

Thanks for reading **Axel**!

Want to see what happens when Kelly, the curvy cafe owner falls for single daddy shifter Bane, literally?

When an unlucky tumble takes her off her feet, Bane, and his adorable toddler, Ollie, step in to help with the cafe. But while Kelly is on the mend, she starts to have her suspicions about some shady activity across the street. Can she resist the call of Bane's animal magnetism long enough to solve the mystery, or is it just her imagination getting the best of her?

Find out in **Bane: Single Daddy Shifters #2.**

Keep reading for a sample, or grab your copy now:

https://www.tashablack.com/singledaddyshifters.html

BANE - SAMPLE

1

KELLY

Kelly McDermott gazed out the window at her approaching quarry.

Minna Randolf was practically trotting toward the shop. The older woman was wearing a sweatshirt with kittens on it today. Her ample bosoms made the friendly felines seem to nod emphatically with each step.

Kelly glanced down her wares one last time.

Everything was in order. The muffins in the baskets were lined up like soldiers, juicy blueberries and coffeecake toppings proudly on display. The bagels leaned on each other in long rows, showing off, swirls of rye, seas of sesame seeds and crinkly onion bits. Stainless steel urns of fragrant flavored coffee lined the counter top.

And under the glass case, in the center of a circle of bear claws was the pièce de résistance - a mountain of fragrant cinnamon buns, their glaze glistening in the morning light.

Kelly sighed with satisfaction.

She had to be up before five every day to make it happen, but *Mornings at McDermott's* was ready for business.

Kelly had always dreamed of having a book and bake

shop. When this space had opened up just after her grandmother left her a tidy sum of inheritance money, she figured it was meant to be.

For now, the books on the built-in shelves Jack Harkness had installed for her were all Kelly's own - free for any customer to borrow.

But one day she hoped to make the place a real bookshop, where local authors could come in to do readings and sell their work.

Outside, Minna had almost reached the shop.

Kelly couldn't help noticing the worried look on her favorite customer's face. Minna was glancing at her watch, almost as if she were late.

Kelly wasn't sure how you could be late to grab a cinnamon bun and curl up with a good book, but it was the only way to explain Minna's expression.

Then it happened.

Minna turned and went into the storefront across the street.

Kelly's mouth dropped open in horror.

Et tu, Minna?

But she had seen it with her own eyes.

Minna was going straight in the door of *Yoga Valhalla*.

Kelly sighed and looked around her café.

It was empty.

And it looked like it was going to stay that way a little while longer.

Ever since Whitney Ogden had opened *Yoga Valhalla* right across the street, no one seemed to want to buy artisanal baked goods and chocolates anymore.

And it made a certain kind of sense.

The gigantic windows of the yoga studio had a direct view into the café. Kelly figured her customers must feel

guilty for luxuriating in good old-fashioned carbs and litera-
ture in front of their fitness-minded friends.

Kelly had nothing against good exercise, she enjoyed a
nice long walk every evening herself. But she couldn't deny
that this particular studio in this particular location was
making things harder for her.

Fall was typically Kelly's busy season. Off-routine moms
getting their kids off to school would stop in for a store-
bought pick-me-up, and if they enjoyed the experience, pick
up a new habit that involved books and baked goods.
Deeper into the season, shoppers would stop in for a quick
bite and a gift card.

Her slowest time was normally January when so many
people were still trying to stick to their New Year's reso-
lutions.

But if things kept up like this, she might not make it
until January.

At least she still had one regular customer she could
count on. Well, two...

She smiled to herself as she headed back to the kitchen,
thinking of Bane Wilson and his son Ollie.

When Kelly bought the building, she'd been excited
about the two apartments above the shop. She would have
one for herself and the other would make an amazing guest
suite for visiting authors one day.

But the last six months after the yoga studio opened had
been lean, and she'd decided to rent out the other apartment to help her business stay afloat.

Dulcie Blanco of Tarker's Hollow Realty Group found
her a perfect tenant at a rent so high Kelly worried it might
be unethical.

"There aren't too many rentals in Tarker's Hollow, so it's
simple supply and demand," Dulcie explained. "And Bane

has plenty of money. He just needs a place for himself and Oliver while they wait for the big house to sell."

Bane Wilson was kind of a legend in Tarker's Hollow - at least among book nerds like Kelly and her friends. Popular and athletic in high school, but always polite and friendly, Bane had gone on to a high-profile career as a literary agent out in Glacier City.

But when his sister and her husband died in a car accident, Bane gave it all up to move back to Tarker's Hollow and raise his nephew, Oliver, in his home community.

Bane wasn't even keeping the house - an exquisitely renovated and gargantuan stone center hall colonial up on Elm Avenue. Rumor had it that his plan was to find a nice little cottage in the center of town and put the proceeds from the sale of the big old house into a college account for Ollie.

Kelly McDermott had been anything but popular in high school. The curves she had grudgingly learned to love in adulthood had just cropped up back then. Her petite height made her seem even rounder. And the flashy grill of metal braces made her hide her shy smile.

She knew Bane Wilson was supposed to be a nice guy, but she hadn't exactly run in his circles.

Now that she saw him every day though she had to admit that everyone was right about him - he really was perfect.

But not as perfect as Ollie.

Three years old and full of wonder, Oliver Wilson was the embodiment of Kelly's own spirit. He loved baking, he loved books, and he wore his big heart on his little sleeve.

She adored him and dreaded the day when the two of them would inevitably move on to slightly bigger and much better things.

But until then, she was determined to make life as cheerful for Ollie as possible.

She grabbed the box that had arrived yesterday afternoon out of her little office and headed back into the café to set up. If she was quick, she could get it all done before Ollie got downstairs.

2

BANE

Bane Wilson tried not to smile as he faced off with his adversary.

"*No,*" Ollie said, the word somewhat muffled by his favorite dinosaur mask.

"Now, Ollie," Bane said reasonably. "We've talked about this before. You can't wear a costume to pre-school."

"Why not?" the small dinosaur demanded, stomping its mighty foot.

"Well, for one thing your teacher might get confused," Bane said. "*Where is Ollie? Is he lost?*" His imitation of Teacher Helen was pretty good - he'd had plenty of practice. He pretended to look all over the room. "*Oh dear, oh dear, dear, dear...*" He sniffed a little for effect. Ollie loved Teacher Helen.

"I'm here!" Ollie cried, ripping off the mask.

"*Oh, thank heavens,*" Bane said in Teacher Helen's voice.

Ollie wrapped his arms around Bane's waist.

Bane felt the familiar pang of pride and loss.

Ollie was the spitting image of his mother, and Bane's sister, Risa, in moments like this. He missed her exuberance so much, and was very grateful he had this small person to remind him of her.

"That won't *really* happen," Ollie said, sounding a little uncertain. "I can still wear my costume."

"How about a compromise?" Bane suggested.

"Okay," Ollie agreed, amazing Bane.

"Do you remember what a compromise is?" Bane asked.

"Yes," Ollie said seriously. "I get what I want - but only kind of."

"Wow, bud, very good," Bane said, nodding. "How about this compromise? What if you don't wear your dinosaur costume, but you do wear your light-up dinosaur sneakers *and* your dinosaur backpack?"

Ollie considered for a moment.

"Yeah, okay," he said at last, peeling his costume off and leaving it on the floor in a pile.

Bane figured they could focus on cleaning up later. For now the calm negotiation was a victory.

"Great," Bane said. "And look, I even packed you this dinosaur cheese stick for your snack."

He showed Ollie the cheese stick.

"That's not a dinosaur cheese stick," Ollie said. "That's just a regular cheese stick."

"Not if you eat it like *this*," Bane said. "*Rawwwrrrrrr.*"

He pretended to gobble up the cheese stick while holding it with tiny T-Rex hands.

Ollie's laughter was like a waterfall.

"Are you ready to walk to pre-school?" Bane asked.

"Yes," Ollie said.

"Are your shoes on?"

"Yes."

"Backpack on?"

"Yes."

"*Yes*," Bane said. "Let's do it."

They headed out of the apartment together and down the narrow staircase.

Ollie walked ahead, obligingly holding the handrail even though it was high for him. Another compromise, because he didn't want to have to hold Bane's hand every time.

"Good morning, Ollie," Kelly's voice sang out when they reached the café below.

She was bent over something in the corner near the glass case, but she stood and waved to Ollie.

"Hi, Kelly, I'm hungry," Ollie said, unsubtly angling for a treat from their friendly landlady.

"I was hoping you might say that," Kelly said. "I made something new this morning and I need someone to try it out."

"Me," Ollie cried, delighted. "I will try it!"

"Thank you, Ollie," Kelly said.

Bane watched as she scurried off behind the counter.

Kelly McDermott had been the quiet type in high school. Bane remembered her as forever awkward, hiding behind that silky cascade of hair.

The soft hair was back in a ponytail today, so he could see her heart-shaped face. She had blossomed into a beautiful woman who was right at home in her own skin.

And she was especially beautiful when she was talking with Ollie.

"Okay," she said, carrying a small bag. "You know how sometimes you want to try a muffin, but it's too big?"

Ollie knew about that. He nodded enthusiastically.

"These are mini-muffins," Kelly said. "This way you can try three different muffins and they are the right size."

"Oh," Ollie said, his eyes sparkling as he examined the bag of small muffins.

"Give them a try, and tell me if you like them when you get home from school okay?" Kelly asked. "I put them in a bag in case you wanted to have some for your snack."

"I swear I feed him," Bane told her quietly.

She smiled up at him, eyes sparkling, and he felt something shift in his chest, a whisper of excitement.

The wolf inside him pricked up his ears and tasted her scent. She was exquisite.

Mine.

"You're a great dad," she told him, blissfully unaware of the effect she was having on his wolf. "I just like giving him a little treat. I hope it's okay."

"It's more than okay," Bane said, forcing himself to look away from her.

He glanced down at Ollie, who was already sampling a mini muffin and making happy humming sounds as he chewed, cheeks puffed out like a chipmunk.

"You'd better go," Kelly said. "I don't want to make you guys late."

"Sure," he said reluctantly. "See you later."

They waved good-bye to her and then headed out.

Bane took a deep breath of the cool fall air to center himself.

It was overcast, the damp air saturating the colors of the small town: slate gray sidewalk festooned with fiery fallen leaves, bright shop signs, and the glistening yellows and scarlet leaves still whispers on the tree branches in the wind.

The scent of rain was on the air and Bane could practically feel the sizzle of lightning.

Or maybe it was just the aftereffects of his interaction with Kelly.

"I think it's going to rain today, bud," Bane told Ollie, putting himself back into dad-mode. "You still have your jacket in your backpack, right?"

"Right," Ollie said through a mouthful of muffin.

"Good work," Bane told him. "How's the muffin."

"Great," Ollie squeaked.

"Kelly's a good baker," Bane said.

"Mm," Ollie agreed around his next bite.

They walked on, crossing Yale and passing the community center.

"Playgroup," Ollie said, casually pointing at the building on his way past.

"Yup," Bane agreed.

The pre-school was just on the other side of the parking lot.

Normally there was a tangle of cars at the drop-off and the shouts of children on tricycles and playing in the sandbox.

But the place was empty - no cars, no kids, no barricades out.

"Not again," Bane groaned, pulling out his phone.

The pre-school was the best in the area, but they were closed for every conceivable holiday known to man.

"Nobody's here," Ollie said sadly.

"It must be Talk-Like-a-Pirate Day or something," Bane said, scrolling through his phone to see if he had an email about it.

"It *is?*" Ollie asked excitedly.

"Oh, I was only kidding, bud," Bane said. "But you can talk like a pirate if you want."

"I'll talk like a dinosaur," Ollie decided. "*Rawrrrr!*"

Bane smiled and roared back.

Yup, there was the email. The pre-school was closed today for staff reinvigoration - whatever that was. It was even in his calendar.

Bane sighed.

Though he knew he was doing his best in his new role as a dad, and trying to accustom himself to his new lifestyle, this was a proof positive that he was still overwhelmed and having a hard time staying organized.

"Let's go home," he told Ollie. "I think it's going to start raining soon."

"Can we go to the library?" Ollie asked.

"Sure," Bane told him. "But let's do that after I have my coffee."

"That's a good compromise," Ollie announced and stomped off toward the shop, looking down at his little feet every few steps to admire the lights on his sneakers.

Bane thought about his plan for the day. BuzzLine was looking for top ten lists and he'd had one in mind to throw together today while Ollie was at school. He wondered if he could get it done during the nap.

Freelance writing had been his first gig out of college - it put food on his table while he did an unpaid internship at Glacier City Press that led to getting on the acquisitions team. From there he'd made the connections that lead to him acting as a literary agent to one rising star and then another.

It was a little odd to be back to writing blog posts. But the beauty of it was that anyone could do it for quick money.

He wrote them under a pen name so no one had to know that Bane Wilson was completely out of the publishing game.

Though he knew that as long as he was living in Tarker's Hollow, it was unlikely he'd be working in publishing again.

He had plenty of savings - his own, and Risa's, which she had left to him.

But it didn't feel right to spend it. As far as he was concerned, that money really belonged to Ollie.

Spending money on the apartment rental while they waited for the house to sell was one thing. The child psychologist had told him it would be ideal if Ollie could have a fresh start and didn't have to think about new people coming into his house. The apartment would be a great place for them to transition into their new lives together.

But beyond that, Bane liked working and wanted to add to their fortunes, not subtract from them.

"You're back," Kelly exclaimed as Ollie threw open the door to the café, sending the bells above jangling.

"Pre-school is *closed*," Ollie said. "It's Talk-Like-a-Dinosaur Day! *Rawwrrr!*"

"That's really awesome," Kelly said. "Because I have a surprise for you."

"You do?" Ollie looked like he had won the lottery.

"Well, it's not just for you, it's for any kids who come into the café with their grown-ups," Kelly amended.

Bane was grateful for the easy way she had said "with their grown-ups" not "with their parents." Ollie was Bane's son now by adoption, but he still remembered his daddy, and Bane never wanted that to change.

Ollie followed Kelly over to the corner where a small wooden table with three chairs was set up.

On the table was a deluxe set of crayons in a massive box, and beside it, a stack of coloring and activity books.

The one on top had a picture of a roaring T-rex.

"Wow," Ollie cried, pulling out a chair and getting right down to business.

Kelly smiled down at him fondly and Bane felt the flames licking at his heart.

Mine, the wolf growled.

"Thank you," Bane said, ignoring the wolf. "That's really nice of you."

"I figure this way maybe you can get a cup of coffee and relax for a minute," Kelly said.

"Coffee sounds great," he said. "And maybe I can get a few minutes of work done."

"Go grab your laptop," Kelly told him. "I'll keep an eye on Ollie."

"Thank you," he told her, heading for the stairs before they could make eye contact and send the wolf into a frenzy again.

He didn't know why his inner wolf had been so crazy around her lately, but if the beast had to lose its marbles, at least it was for someone nice like Kelly McDermott.

***

Want to find out what happens when Bane and Kelly suddenly become a whole lot closer? Are you ready for some steamy connections, a heated rivalry, a late night mystery, and more adorable Ollie?
Then grab your copy now!
Bane: Single Daddy Shifters #2.

https://www.tashablack.com/singledaddyshifters.html

TASHA BLACK STARTER LIBRARY

Packed with steamy shifters, mischievous magic, billionaire superheroes, and plenty of HEAT, the Tasha Black Starter Library is the perfect way to dive into Tasha's unique brand of Romance with Bite!

Get your FREE books now at tashablack.com!

ABOUT THE AUTHOR

Tasha Black lives in a big old Victorian in a tiny college town. She loves reading anything she can get her hands on, writing paranormal romance, and sipping pumpkin spice lattes.

Get all the latest info, and claim your FREE Tasha Black Starter Library at www.TashaBlack.com

Plus you'll get the chance for sneak peeks of upcoming titles and other cool stuff!

Keep in touch...
www.tashablack.com
authortashablack@gmail.com

facebook.com/romancewithbite
twitter.com/romancewithbite

Made in the USA
Las Vegas, NV
20 December 2022